57 Octaves Below Middle C

Also by Kevin McIlvoy

A Waltz
The Fifth Station
Little Peg
Hyssop
The Complete History of New Mexico

57 Octaves Below Middle C

Kevin McIlvoy

Four Way Books
Tribeca

Please direct all inquiries to:
Editorial Office
Four Way Books
POB 535, Village Station
New York, NY 10014
www.fourwaybooks.com

Library of Congress Cataloging-in-Publication Data

Names: McIlvoy, Kevin, 1953- author.
Title: 57 octaves below middle C / Kevin McIlvoy.
Other titles: Fifty-seven octaves below middle C
Description: New York : Four Way Books, [2017]
Identifiers: LCCN 2017000675 | ISBN 9781935536987 (softcover : acid-free paper)
Classification: LCC PS3563.C369 A6 2017 | DDC 813/.54--dc23
LC record available at https://lccn.loc.gov/2017000675

This book is manufactured in the United States of America and printed on acid-free paper.

Four Way Books is a not-for-profit literary press. We are grateful for the assistance
we receive from individual donors, public arts agencies, and private foundations.

This publication is made possible with public funds from the New York State Council on the Arts,
a state agency.

We are a proud member of the Community of Literary Magazines and Presses.

Distributed by University Press of New England
One Court Street, Lebanon, NH 03766

Mom,
you would not have liked this one at all. Still, you would have listened in
loving puzzlement to every note of the music. You would have offered me
the music of your cleansing and crossing-all-distances laughter, still. Here
it is, then—
in memory of you.

Contents

Basho, poet, diarist, recluse, sells lawn mower—used but like new 3

Miss Luck 10

Session 5 17

Road Open—Gone Soon 22

Black sweater 24

The Luthier's mother's mouth's openness 26

At dusk, as always, Bender sang to us 28

The thing—the foot ruler thing—in the shoe store—it tells your size? I can't remember what it is called. What is it called? 31

I was watching the movie, edited 32

Ladies Room 34

Veterans Day 42

November 22 50

A word to Teacher Reptile's readers and their parents on the occasion of Father's Day and the anniversary of Teacher Reptile's release from Eight Gates Correctional Facility 61

When will we speak of Jesus? 68

All of the stones all at the same time 76

Mrs. Wiggins' altocumulus undulatus asperatus 85

A testicular self-examination 90

Notes on his poems by a guy who observed them in their natural habitat. 95

The last things we said 96

Oh, how glad and happy when we meet 104

"On the wire, Boys." 111

A 4 oz. can of story   112

An 8 oz. can of story   114

The Y   116

On a dare he gave himself   120

19th & Minnesota   122

The nature of the business in Extraellaville   129

The story of their 67th   131

I'll go home after this. Right after this. I promise.   134

Shaken protest departure from local asylum   137

Visiting privileges at Les Gauld Motors, downtown Ellaville   140

Greetings from Teacher Reptile on the occasion of Father's Day and the publication of the final volume of *The Wrath* septology   142

New Year's Eve, my brother monk, eleven miles apart from me, in his thirty-second year at Lady Mori's Garden Soto Zen Temple in Wendellton, North Carolina, sends annual text, "How was 2014?"   146

When I would take it from him there was the problem   148

Hitchhiker, Seedvul, North Carolina, asked by the driver, "Where to?"   149

Bright-Very   150

The color in the bed of the river? You wonder, What is it?   151

You are the best audience we have ever had.   152

And after these cries, I, Teacher Reptile, heard a dementer on the bank say to me from the lake of fire, "This is the second death" and "Here there shall be more pain"   155

Perfumery   159

You want to know—   162

Aisle 4, Mini Bob's Mart   165

Batter   166

Basho, poet, diarist, recluse, sells lawn mower — used but like new

> Like-new *karumi*.
> 2-stroke. Kireji design.
> Make an offering.

I had phoned, not sure I needed another lawnmower, but you never do know, and I lived alone, and living alone like that, I thought lawnmowers were unchanging truths. Like other men I was drawn to them, seriously drawn, so I had them. Where a car might be parked, or chairs and tables and children's outgrown shoes and clothes stored, I had them everywhere, seriously, everywhere.

He answered the phone, "Basho!"

I told him I read the *Thrifty Nickel*, asked if he still had the *karumi*, still wanted to sell. Yes, he did, he had, how pleased he was that I read his simple ad, he said, and it would not "disturb" if I came in the evening when he and his "disciples," who had gathered at his "hut" (his words: hut, disciples, disturb), would "demonstrate *karumi*."

It all was intriguing, it was strange, but, strangely, not surprising from the start: a guy in a hut with his own demonstrating disciples. An ad for a *karumi*. A *karumi*! And I had lawnmowers, I had many, enough, enough that, after years of collecting, I was pleased with every mower. But I had no *karumi*, manufactured by the Dogen Company in '67, designed by Kireji, discontinued in the '70s. *Karumi Kan!* was the TV campaign.

There was more I was trying to remember about the skillful means of *karumi* when I drove out of the city, up to his place. I drove across an arched wooden bridge to an adobe hut in the middle of a large lawn—the wrong lawn for our long New Mexico drought. Next to the hut was a tree with giant leaves, and, under it, shovelheads of sunset shade, and in them what you'd have to, should, might call disciples. I took off my straw mowing hat, breathed out, breathed out, said my name, said, "I'm Wallace," to all of them. Disciples. Seriously.

The four of them sang it back like a chorus of frogs. "Wall-less!

3

Wall-less!"

And my own name was all I needed in order to breathe in, to remember more then about that TV ad: *Karumi Kan! Karumi Kan!* whooped blissfully by gray and white cranes pushing mowers with their wingtips over blocks and blocks of city lawns. A close view of their knotted long legs, and the big paper boats of their bodies. The long view of them, a kinship of hundreds of thousands. The view from heaven of mown lawns, dewy and glistening. Finally, just the word, *karumi*, all lowered lower-case. Pulsing, vibrating, like an opening lotus. *karumi*. Like the engine of a calm mind. And from the machine of the one word: the clipping sound, beyond cessation.

He wheeled it out from behind his fragile hut. If he pushed his feet against any wall it might collapse. A little monk-like, this guy, he squinted the way monks do in Disney. It had to be him. Basho. He held the mower handle with one hand. He pinched his hat brim. At first, he didn't look at me. His mineral-blue eyes made a pass over every fresh blade of the fescue around him. He bent over to look at but see no farther than what was the way between distant and close. He wavered, he nearly tipped over, nearly tipped up. Seriously, what was I supposed to make of that?

I almost spoke to the mower. I felt I already had Basho's invitation.

He said, "You are here at last—the moon, rusting red, follows—my correct address!"

The co-arising words and the silences were like shallow cups poured full and taken someplace far away to be emptied and brought back over a great distance before being poured full from other cups.

We looked over the mower, like two men in a mirror, one pushing his face forward, the other back, and only so much room. Clean mower—like you'd expect of this man in a clean white terrycloth bathrobe with a wide black band around it.

4

Clean mower, I said to it, inside myself, of course, because that's why I had them, so many mowers—to privately talk to. Clean mower, I said. I felt as unworded as in my dreams.

The disciples of Basho left the shade of the tree. They formed a playground line. Close. You know the kind: hands on each other's shoulders. Grown men.

Basho said, "The tall grasses bend—hours and hours of relenting—making offerings."

He pulled the starter cord, he set the lever from the sign of the turtle to the sign of the rabbit. When he placed his hands on the T-shaped handle, the disciples bowed and bowed and bowed, nine slow prostrations, and stood. Basho moved the handle towards Wright, who bowed again, a determined bow that was in the man's nature now, no matter what his nature once had been.

He cut the first, the outermost, circle, and bestowed the *karumi* to the next, Shiki, who faithfully made a path partly inside that smooth path, and passed it to the next, Issa, and the smiling next, Buson. The disciples introduced themselves: Buson softly said, "Buson," and took my hands into his and turned them up and over as if washing them in his gaze; Issa put his face very close to the closed bud of my hands in the cradle of Buson's; Shiki stood near, said nothing; and the determined man, the one I had met first, said, "He's Shiki, I'm Wright—I love saying that! Give him his hands back now, Buson."

A little doubtfully, Buson handed me back that part of myself as if it was still mine. It was, of course, but for a second there I had forgotten that. I recognized Wright as somebody with the name tag "Richard," a clerk at the Kmart.

When I said so, he said, "Known as the Big K—lovely,

appealing features—but: Martha Stewart."

"Right," I said to Wright, to Richard, in order to delight him. Do you see that already I had changed into my hands? Mine—and then, lost in the giving of them, not mine. I knew I had seen Issa and Shiki at the Target department store, place of many afflictions and wisdoms. The Lawn and Garden Department. Buson, I learned later, owned The **tzu-jan** Nursery on Highway 28 near Vado. He sold flowers and, with full flats of them, he gave away goldfinches. I have his handwritten poster: *Goldfinches inside—hold one and you will decide. They already know.*

Look, I could see, I can see, seriously now—this was pretty clearly a mowing cult. They—cults—found me those days. And that wasn't a bad thing. I was more ready for Basho than I thought.

Half an hour of mowing passed, but it felt like only an instant. Instantly, the bowing blades of grass stood straight, the bag swelled: side-carriage, pure duck cloth, green-striped white. The rain-smell of freshcut rose from the earth. The disciples, now holding each other's hands like small boys, looked within from within. They stood in a circle with a broken space where I could stand.

At the tree, Basho slowly circled, cutting not quite close enough around. On the handle his slight, closed fists subtly jumped like hatching chrysalises.

He finished.

He handed me the *karumi.* Kireji design. The T-handle painted, lacquered a pearl cloisonné color. Before I even pushed, I felt: Lightness! Lightness!

Quiet-running. You can talk to a mower when it's still. When it's running what is there? No matter how ready you are, the hard thing to accept is that you have nothing to say—nothing. Seriously. Nothing.

I halved the path Basho had halved of his disciples' paths. Circling smartly, smoothly around the tree trunk, the point of origination, I said inside myself, Clean mower! Work done! Asking me nothing, nothing—no answering song.

On Buson's instructions, each of us mowed a ray from the Basho tree to the outer edge of the circle we had made. A wheel. Seven spokes.

People want to know how I came to live in this isolated falling-apart hut near the Rio Grande, which flows towards but no longer finds the ocean. A lawn boy at the age of fifty-four. Pushing my mower over this small wooden bridge, and going into the world to mow, and keeping my shift as groundskeeper at the Big K, too, and leaving that world to push my mower back.

I needed to mow. I needed the right mower. Many of us do.

Have you ever seen cranes kettling? By the hundreds, by the tens of thousands, they circle upward, slower, higher, rising into a galaxy shape. And, over many hours, it feels like eons, the circling becomes a churning.

And a single crane falls out of that open sleeve. And down. It pulls the other cranes after it in a fast-spinning unthreading. And you see a shallow funnel form that deepens until it has a wide lip, a throat, a bottom tip. A tornado of cranes.

When I said I would buy the mower, Basho nodded to his disciples, who bowed their necks, who seemed emptied, or their eyes did, or their bony shoulders, or their shorn heads. They retreated, returned with shovels, including one for me.

By now it was late. Evening. The moon, through the darkening clouds, burned.

We dug.

We wounded the roots the way you have to when you tear something from all its attachments. Wright recited a prayer, "O, child of noble birth, do not be afraid, do not be afraid of what you remember, do not be afraid of what you forget. Do not be afraid. Do not be afraid. Do not." We said nothing. But, inside us, we recited the weird prayer after him.

We sat down.

Basho left, walking on the spokepath that led to his hut. He brought hot water that he poured into a clay bowl with powder at the bottom.

The steam burnished the goldening air around us. We passed the bowl. Buson, Issa, Shiki, and Wright each held it up to the tree's branches before they drank. When the bowl got to me, the sharp green smell poked me in the eyes and made me slightly woozy. I giggled, and they all spontaneously giggled with me, once and all at once.

Our warmed hands held the trunk of the tree. It almost seemed to help us lift it from its home.

Basho explained to me that this was the fourth transplanting.

And now he was taking it away again. And only it.

He asked if I felt it clinging. I did not.

Our faces and hands grew cool—our eyes and our throats.

The next morning Buson laid a harp of jonquils on the slight depression in the earth. He left that day. Issa and Shiki stayed a week. Before Wright moved on, he helped me bring a few things here from my home in town.

I took Wright into the triple-wide garage, showed him my mowers.

Wright croaked, "Wallace! Wallace!"

Twenty-eight lawnmowers, each one uniquely itself. My first bought when I was twenty-eight.

At auction, we started them all up and left them running. The radiating noise and the fuel odor and the pointlessness of the blades slicing air made the bidding go high, the final offers higher. As each one was sold, we full-throttled the engine to the sign of the rabbit; slowly, slowly down-throttled to the sign of the turtle; turned the machine off, and transmitted it to its new owner. We bowed.

Miss Luck

I was howling when I left my house on August first, a Friday, one a.m., my children asleep and haunted wife snoring, and went out into the warm, hard rain in only my boxers to howl more, to circle my block and bow at every neighbor's yard and vomit.

I was vomiting and weeping, and wiping drool on my bare arms and biting into my hairy wrists, and blowing myself and my day-old donuts out on Red and Recita's yard, and ornamenting the bushes of the kindest elderly lesbian couple we had known for ten years but whose names I never learned, two lovely women, waitresses at El Patio Bar & Grill, whose sweet-smelling rose bushes helped me gag up more of what I needed to be rid of. Creamed beef. Creamed baked potatoes. Creamed cheese and macaroni, green pear, green hockers of ham fat. Creamed running shoes, I think, or something looking like shoetongue or shoestring.

I whimpered my migraine's name, Miss Luck, and wiped creamed corn chips and blood (or blood-sauced Chachi's salsa) from my legs, and I gave thanks for the rain washing my face and my feet and the moon—not much of a moon to speak of—and, yes, I have a name for the migraine suffering visiting me since I was ten and seizures first made the brainshear that welcomed the lightning that invited in the blessed kindness named Miss Luck.

Oh, Miss Luck, I said, welcome back! You look devastating. You look like every boyman's dream of a creepy woman parting his mind's curtains. You are the second-best worst creamed thing I can imagine, oh, my migraine, oh my hellkite crone, oh Death's substitute teacher with no syllabus, no lasting respect for your students but with Death's school spirit, her bifocals, bad gums, her pink and yellow chalk, cruel pop tests, and two absolute rules: Shut up. Shut up.

I was trying to shut up my moaning when I got down on all fours, doglike, and couldn't get up, and composted Mrs. Armendarez's irises with the carne adovada I had eaten on Wednesday. Mrs. A and her two sisters, having outlived their total of seven husbands, lived to tell what gross medical invasions each herself and her sisters had survived, and lived to love each other better, they said, without saying better than what. Or maybe they said than what—even upright and on two legs, I hadn't listened. And they potted, they potted cherry tomatoes and strawberry eggplants and rose peppers. Their windowsills and walks were lined with the potted, and in their front and back yard were irises, all kinds. No lawns, no hedges, no fences, no mowers, no men.

I swayed over the green iris spears and the open soft blue iris blooms, and drops of golden iris dust dripped from the nest of hair on my belly. A migraine dog, an alley mutt, I moaned in wondrous pain, the suffering that surpasses all understanding, when Miss Luck casts demons in, maketh the lame men lamer, and blinds again the healed blind.

Mrs. A's light went on. Her hunched, restless shadow and the two siblings of it spread that familiar stain of the incomprehensible across her kitchen wall. I growled, "You bitches," and trotted on all fours into the dark alley behind me, and looked up the length of it. I thought I saw the colors of young girls' painted lips on the puddles. I shook myself and shivered and wagged my butt to empty water from my sloshy boxers.

I pawed one of the lovely broths of vomit. Something floated there, a floating masticated, acrid, half-creamed uncanned meal. Buoyant. I sniffed, I lapped up some, upchucked, and lapped, gorged, gagged. Against one alley cinderblock wall I sniffed him-it, sensed how him-man-it he was. Saw.

A mandogman. Never had I seen one, not one, in so many raining migraine nights of roaming.

Dog. Man.

He nodded his wide jaw at me, his mouth closed, back lowered. Bigger than me. He lumbered out of the wall's shadow. Wide, white-haired shoulders. BVDs wash-machine pink. Ears weedy with white-gray hairs. His mouth and nose leaked.

"I'm glad I don't have that," I said. Human, I would have said something else. Human, I would have said, "Are you okay?" I would have asked, "Migraine?"

He said, "Have you?" and splashed into the alley toward me, and brushed himself against me, the bottom end strings will be brushed that way on a guitar and brushed again for the sake of the truth of it, and with his bare flank against my flank, right haunch against my left, he pushed his gray snout at mine and said, "Have you—seen the pack?"

The pack.

"The pack?"

Rain streamed from his balding head, flooded the loose flesh under his eyes, old teen-child-man face. His pale jowls shed rainy sheets of mucus from his pitted nose and mouth. Seventy, I guessed.

"The pack?" I asked.

"Four more," he said. His slack neck and old man's purple dugs swayed, dripped rainwater over a puddle on which wind smoothed the picture of him-dog him-man and swicked it off again. "My eyes can't tolerate—" he whispered, showed me collapsing pink branches across blasted eyes big as pince-nez lenses, "—light."

"Light," he repeated, his legs and bare front feet anointed with drainage.

"Be straight with me," I said in order to undog him.

Like any man in enough good pain, he wouldn't undog. He heeled, said, "I lost," glanced up the alley, "them," and rang his head, and closed his lids, and groaned. I thought, Where does he think we are— what does he think I am? But I could already answer.

I groaned with him, shut my own awnings, listened to rain hiss over us, swallowed a reflux scone of phlegm, and said, I am so grateful, Miss Luck, for this nightmare—and for the heat flashing inside the slipstream of my skin where (I hope I am mistaken, Miss Luck, I hope I am) this old hound or man seems to have *licked my face.*

"Clean," he said. And licked. Not a rude tongue, not unknowing or insincere.

"There," he said, rain churning through the jagged seams of his naked skull. "There. They are."

They are? They are.

They were. There.

Four more men loping forward on all fours. Four soaked heads hanging, and backs slumped. Four crawling silhouettes of misery, the four alleydogs of the apocalypse, well, six if you include Mr. Lick and me, which you must, you must, since I was welcomed to the pack just like that. This is how easily men will accept men who are, in one way or another, dogs.

"This yours?" asked José Geisel, nose-nudging some floating vomit-candied chicken mole near my knees.

"José?" I asked. I knew the man from church, his sons knew mine from school, our wives were friends at work. José. Dog. Lawyer.

I said the chicken wasn't mine. Lick said, "José's yankin'. Your tail."

I didn't ask, What tail?

"I'm Seuss," said one of them, probably thirty, thirty-five, someone I'd never met, and introduced himself as José's oldest son, as the one from his father's first marriage, and then he nudged at the other two old, old wiseguys. Dos and Tres were their mutt names, he said. He explained that our neighborhood was not their turf but they came when the rain and the aura of the migraine or the call from the pack reached them in a dream.

They didn't sniff me, but they sniffed me out, if you know what

I mean, and you do if you have the luck to have Miss Luck and you're a dogmangoddogman with your cooked brains caught fire, slouching out of or toward some neighborhoodwoman's yard at an obscene hour to puke and howl in a pack of men pulling a sleigh full of prostration.

We loped. To the corner of Mangor and Bekin, past the posted signs for the Neighborhood Watch, past the distended chain-link fences, the dark open mouths of the mailboxes, over the top of the crumbling concrete curbs, to the top of the earth in heaps at the site of the sewer repair, to the broken brick girdle around the home of Gladys Lembethem who had no motion-detector lamps, no gardens, no trees, no gun, no pots, no pissed-off screaming realdog dogs.

We were away from everything and everyone but each other when we crouched in the mud of Lembethem and pressed our rumps to the ground, and rose and backpedaled and did the stadium-style Dog Wave almost twice, and sat and groaned together intimately, intimately and unselfconsciously, the way a pack of men will never do unless they think of you, Miss Luck, and think of women's mouths and their wet or wetlook gloss lips, all the Miss Lucks they knew through all the years, and contemplate what medicines they took for all that and where and how they vomited them up—the exact texture, heat, and taste.

"Haaa-ooooooh!" I screamed, and the ice-axe blood in my belly and head spoke for me, and the pack echoed that, and one of them, probably Seuss, said, "*What*—" and Mr. Lick said, "—is it?" And there was a solemn canine expectant silence.

"Miss Luck! Miss Luck!" I raised my paw, raised it higher to be seen among all the questioning, answering men at our assigned seats. "I can answer!" I said. I knew I could. Oh, Miss Luck, tide crushing what it uncovers, nest built for the ruthless, bread that wounds the knife, oh, Miss Luck, I thought, this is a test I have already taken. I know how to

14

take it and be good. Uncalled upon, I told what truth I knew men in pain trust first.

"Women's lips," I said. Human, I would have said, "Look at us. Six pissbuckets, six sicknesses, six mopped-up sacks of vomit-soaked sawdust, six of Miss Luck's awful teacher's pets." I said, instead, "Women's lips."

Dos and Tres, shorthairs, big translucent ears, dark, clotted eyes—their own lips kind of red-cracked black—yipped.

Seuss yipped, laughed, said back to me, "Okay then. Women's lips."

The rain-splattered mud made flapping, hissing noises around us. How hungry the act and the art of remembering can make a mutt! Dreamily, Lick said, "Yep," and sneezed, and convulsed, and leaked a spinachy trickle from his snout, and said, "Lips."

The penetrating rain in the thought of this, of their lips, young girls', young women's and women's lips, pelted, defeated, quieted, kenneled, calmed us.

Lick's nosebleed slowed.

Tres pawed the tattoo of an ice cream truck riding up his right forearm toward his heart. José, resting on his hindquarters, nudged his glasses up his nose, adjusted the stems behind his ears, wiped tears and rain from the swollen chins under his chin. "Ohhhhh. And women's toes," he said, stricken.

"Hard," said Lick, "to love," and barked out wet splinters of Bermuda grass, and said, "their toes."

"Even when they paint them," said Dos or Tres, their heads tilted toward Lick.

"They don't know what to do with them, do they?" asked Seuss.

I imagined our wives sliding their feet out of the bed sheets and into slippers. "Goodness," I said, "they must know by now we're missing. They're missing us, reporting us lost."

"Not mine," said Dos.

"Don't know," said Tres and Seuss.

And José said, "Not"—and "Mine" said Lick.

We lifted our ashen chests, lifted our heads, lifted our snouts toward our silent houses. It was as if we could see clocks and watchers, hear dreamers hissing and falling. In the air was the taste of birds gutted by lightning, of stripped wires sparking.

"Are there?" I asked.

"Other packs?" asked Lick.

The whole pack madly barked and bit at my elbows and back and hips to warn me: Dangerous!

"Okay," I said, "all right then," picturing legions of wandering dogmen returning to their homes.

We rested. Rested and talked. With our dull, nicked machetes of talk we chopped brush and underbrush of hypothalamus away. We learned we had the same worms in our eyes and mouths and hearts as in our bowels and brains, same heated pus in our ears as in our teeth, same dog shame and dog will wagging the dog wanting a piece of truth to fetch and chew and bring back the you inside him, Miss Luck.

We dwelt upon you in our conversation, we growled about your toes and your dry, wrinkled heels, and your mouths and lips, for hours and hours, until we saw lights come on in the dark houses around us. Women we knew, should know, had known but had ignored or had forgotten, roamed the empty halls and rooms, and knelt in naked pain, and under pain's rule fell to all fours, and under its spell unlocked themselves, and over its threshold ran, and summoned other women—not to search for us men or for their stepfathers, fathers, grandfathers, or their grown sons or brothers, or for any man they once hoped might become another kind, but to gaze out at the rain to seek, as fortune would have it, the rain.

Session 5

for Jonathan Bennett Bonilla and Jeremy Bass

"You—are having a thought?" asked Dr. Darshan's assistant.

"Yes," the client answered. The sensors adhering to the back of the client's head lightly rattled.

"*Stop,*" said Dr. Darshan. She pointed her pencil at the indicators below the rapidly fading digital-image meadow on the computer monitor. The full red bar graph pulsed as its level rose. The diminished blue and green bars barely moved.

The client was having a feeling.

The client often had a feeling at 22-36 Hz resembling an inhibited thought in the 4-7 Hz range. In order to reward the 15-18 Hz range, region 8R of the parietal and region 3R of the temporal should, optimally, produce neither thought nor feeling.

This last of five sessions on 12/31/13 concluded the ninety-session eighteen-month course of neurobiopractice for the client.

During these final sessions the client was, at intervals of 1200 milliseconds, distracted by threshold indications in the 3-bar graph as measured by the troughs and peaks of the 5-band EEG signal.

The client's region 3R and region 8R, experiencing a thought dreaming a feeling, had not completed the virtual meadow, its shading, its color, and its hidden presences in the true measured depth.

Due to the client's emotional instability the volume of meadow audio was set at Constant Zero.

Desiring to complete the meadow, the client concentrated on the outlines of brook and of pendant tree branch. The client sent in-breath through the bottom of his throat, the back of his

17

lungs and upward, a resting pulse rate of 42, his upper lungs the faint pool into which a blue veil poured, in-breath over the smooth stone and down, the misting field beyond the brook, the hill and saddle of hill in the distance, the lineage of benevolent hemlocks there, mother and father, the vigilant hemlocks, in-breath over the frosted window of his breastbone, the dampening of the curtains of his respiratory system, faint open paths of damp gravel on the brook banks, faint grass surrounding the pool, his belly filling with cooling in-breath, filling to brimming, tipping down, spilling out-breath down, again, to the vague bottom of him.

"At Are," said Dr. Darshan's assistant, studying her own computer monitor. When Total Reward was Adequate, she called it to the client's attention, she said, "At Are," shorthand for A-T-R. When Total Reward was Ideal it was I-T-R, designated as "It Are."

A few redbud leaves at a percentage of 6% gray turned cinnamon, their stems almost rain-black, the rest remaining latent, a thought in him again shedding its papery skins, blood coming into the stones in the streambed on the monitor, all of the stones all at the same instant, a pure feeling emerging that the client could not drown, Region 3R a hatch of pale blue duns, Region 8R the last unbound light of stars above the horizon, the morning hovering, the meadow hovering, the client aware of himself as mist in the arms of the hemlocks, hovering arms. Neither a thought nor a feeling. Inside the stream, the form of a white carp, and he the indwelling breeze and he the carp-shadow and rippled pool surface and spilling stream.

"At Are," said Dr. Darshan's assistant, one redbud branch hot with color, the others turning a relative value of 76% shifting into the 80th percentile, lupine crowding the banks, the white flashing inside the carp causing it to tremble, and the client barely breathing, the client breathing, breathed into.

"You—are awake?" Dr. Darshan's assistant asked. "You—are awake? You—are awake?"

Deer Food appeared on the nearest gravelly bank, the client's friend, the beer-gut green squirrel named Deer Food, standing out of balance, facing away from the client. Over his strong gem-green fur shoulder, Deer Food gazed, Deer Food's characteristic drunken gaze, eyes 3% gray, his nicotine-stained darker-green paw out, out and making a request.

"Think me a cigarette, Client. Client? Client: You—are awake? Feel me a light."

Pink Bic lighter. Bubble in the plastic chamber.

Cigarette in his mouth, Deer Food flicked the black trigger.

"And?" Deer Food asked. On Deer Food's loose, knee-length swimming trunks, the perfect spathes of calla lilies.

"At Are," said Dr. Darshan's assistant.

Deer food flicked the trigger once more. White spark.

Blue spark. "And?" Deer Food asked, face vertigo-bright behind the fire.

"At Are," said Dr. Darshan's assistant.

The client's dysregulation mitigated by 18 Hz in region 3R, Deer Foods' cigarette tip catching, his green color and the color of the meadow grass and moss sharpening.

"Kind of you," Deer Food said, drew harder, said, *Mercy.*" The mist behind Deer Food slowly shrugged, the unmoored morning.

"I do not fully appreciate this part," said Deer Food. Crocuses and goldening poppies covered the ground around the client and Deer Food in the next moment, and in the next came the absolute value of sunlit sky, absolute value of stream, of land and fire, the pathways seamless between regions. Reflected in the pool, something arrived, the pattern of waves caused something to arrive: another season, snow cast up from the ground by gusts, snow whirlwinds arising, demons choosing not to kneel.

"It Are," said Dr. Darshan's assistant, reverently.
"It Are," said Dr. Darshan.

Behind Deer Food, at the 18 Hz range, a feeling failing to complete the client's thought, the instantaneously realized body of the frail, hungering creature appeared: the deer.

The deer bowed toward the pool.
It disappeared.

Behind Deer Food, for 480 milliseconds at 15 Hz optimal range, the deer reappeared.
It disappeared.
And, with it, Deer Food.

"You—are having a thought?" Dr. Darshan's assistant asked.
The meadow was drained of all color, the pendant branch entirely withdrawn, the stream a bed of barely visible bloodless stones, the flowering ground gone, the gravelly bank gone, the whiteness of the carp, the carp gone, its lace ghost.
"It's a feeling—a feeling inside a thought," the client

would have said, had he words, to his own reflection on the computer monitor, to Dr. Darshan's assistant, to Dr. Darshan, to the last visible part of the meadow, to the calm omniscient hemlocks.

Road Open—Gone Soon

Stop asking me what I have to show for it, for going out in it
and making a path that disappears behind me and, on the next
shift, disappears before me. Forty-nine years have passed, and
you ask me: Shoveler, Shoveler, is there nothing for you to show
after making white banks on either side of the spine of your
snowbound road? What have you learned that I will learn? What
have you seen that is worthwhile, old shift shoveler? How is
reception there? Is there a signal if you stop at the right place on
your tasks? Do you get message texts?

Voles—their own dream track team—leave their labyrinths in
order to race from where I began to the place of my finish line—
and that cracks me up, but I know you can't say my crack-up is
something to show, something serious. What is more unserious
anyway than a vole drawn out of the darkness by The Shoveler?
The strainings and lungings and the side glances the young wild
offer the wild old ask them to ignore all past warnings. I cause
attentiveness and shrewd pleasure in their black-ice eyes—I am
the treasure that places them in danger.

You have driven past here in the wrong hat and boots for this
weather, have driven past my dark aisle where you have not faced
what is behind the volumes facing out. You'd rather stay in your
rosy warm car inside the margins of the major thoroughfares
salted for you on schedule. Do you have a turn signal, driver? A
single unrestrained impulse? A side or rearview mirror? Forty-
nine years I've been The Shoveler bent over this peculiar whiteness
to make more path beyond what is designated and accustomed.
You will never take the turn in.

This, farther down than you have ever dug, is what I have to show for how I have submitted myself. I have—today—put up a sign.

Black sweater

At the right time in his life, she visited. She apologized that she could stay only briefly. Still: a lucky thing. "Everything in order?" she asked. "Everything done? Good then." And her gray eyes did not meet his. And she did not offer her arms or hands, nor did she look around to find a chair. There was a simple light-green metal chair near the window. Someone had turned it around, tipped it so that it was against the low windowsill where the late afternoon sun exposed the scrapes and chips in the paint.

Her loose slacks, shimmering silver-brown, barely veiled her handsome legs, the cuffs lightly swept over the black hose covering her feet, over the glossy clay-slip color of her high heels.

Her black unbuttoned woman's sweater might've been cashmere or it might have been some other wool, with pearl-white buttons, tiny, positioned impractically near each other, round, clock-pattern buttons, but none near the bottom of her open, light sweater, and none near the scalloped collar. How, he thought, or when would they be buttoned ever?

Couldn't happen: too little material to close over her sheer blouse, white, of course, conch-pink undercolor and coral bra. By now, he thought he might or should feel the old desires, the long thirst. The quiet, small waves he felt would have to be called useless lust.

She asked about other visitors. And about his place. "It's a beautiful place," she said.

What could she mean? Could she mean she wasn't done with remembering? It was as if he'd never before seen a woman's sweater arms not covering her slight wrists, not ending at her elbows either but where, according to some fashion rule, the sweater arms must end: at her mid-forearms, which made him wish she might take it off and become for that one visit not incomprehensible.

Music from down the corridor increased in volume before it went off, not allowed, probably not allowed. The minutes passed as if in one operation of rocking time back and forward and back. She apologized, but she had to leave, she said, and said she knew he understood.

If she only shrugged, the sweater would shift back and its weight rest on her arms and wrists. She could take the material into her smooth fists and tie it round her waist. She could sail it behind her like a bit of twisted sea grass.

He could keep it to himself. He should keep all of it to himself, that the sweater did not reach the middle of her back, did not touch the curve of her hip, that its scalloped neck was lustrous.

He would keep that for himself.

And wasn't it lucky to be a man in an armless man-gown, backless, olive-green, taut blue tie-string, only his thoughts unexposed, a fortunate man to see the back of her woman's sweater as she was leaving, the slightest motion making it swing at that certain place where his arms might have gone.

The Luthier's mother's mouth's openness

The Luthier's mother's mouth's openness, her hands' fingers' tremblings, her red hair's fires' warnings. It's what you saw if you were making your last visit to her ever. You were the Luthier's mother's possession when you walked into her son's guitars' home, in which son and mother also lived together. In one room.

Inside their home's heart's sounds: the tub's faucet's dripping's splashings and the refrigerator's coils' hymning humming and the clock's hands' frettings and the floorboards' one warped floorboard's creaking. It felt like everything you heard was also hearing everything else, that nothing resting there fully rested.

I know all this because I lived there once with an older sister named Bender. She was the one who saw after me. Ran away. And almost no word again from her. My feet drummed the dead forest, I heard my face in the face, and from hunger I prayed inside the box's light. I felt my boy's soul displace the small body of bathtub water. I didn't like that they had stopped that splashing sound.

I was the Luthier's mother's first husband's second child by what people called The Widow's Previous Marriage. The only child left, I was an extraneous adverb when my father, the verb of the family, died. The Luthier, who is the second son, is the Luthier's mother's other.

I, too, was a Luthier though not as skilled as he, The Luthier's Luthier. Call them "Sorrow's sorrows," the guitars I made. Call his "Rapture's Raptures." He was my teacher. Twice his age, I was the Luthier's mother's son's favorite pupil. I was there to learn how to finish Dreadnought-style accoustic guitars that would sell fast. Banking on his reputation, I would claim that he made them.

Once there was one he named Elizabeth Cotton. It is bad luck to name a bad guitar. It is good luck to name a good. He had never made one better. "Liz," he said, at the end, "this will not hurt." And he was gentle. "Liz," he said, "you're going to like this."

He whispered into her soundhole, "Liz, baby, what is it?" and listened for her answer. The Luthier and I never talked with the affection resounding in the Luthier's guitar's conversations with the Luthier. There is a love that is a reflection of love's reflection. There is a frame inside the form, there is a vice you use to force the edges to bind. There is the floating or flying seed still in the grain. The stars arisen, the kingdoms fallen, the green, the void; you touch the tuning fork across the skin of the sky, snow, rain still in the sound. Moonlight. Sun. Nests in the limbs, and in the nests the hungering young. You loosen the vice, and you are done.

"You fixed the tub?" I asked.

The Luthier's mother answered for him: "Fixed."

They had even taken the duct tape off the Hot and Cold handles. (It broke my heart, that repair.)

The Luthier said, "Finished."

I asked if I could take her. Together, the Luthier and I put her in the case.

I left. She went with me everywhere I went. Forty-one years ago today.

At dusk, as always, Bender sang to us

At dusk, as always, Bender sang to our congregation, silver hair greasing her blouse, tin on the toes of her boots.

When we were grade-school children, she and I liked duct tape. We liked it like you could never believe. Our favorite thing to steal from the corner store was that silver coil. The way it ripped across, how it stretched over. It gripped!

She stood on the white twenty-gallon empty drum, her boot heels burning the plastic, her tempo uneven. We were a communion of over a dozen church-bums who loved her and were frightened by her hawk-at-the-tree-crown and hawk-on-the-glide shoulders and head, her wings at her sides, her hands palms out, fingers curled up.

Bender and I once duct-taped a picture of our father, who was dying in the Simic State Penitentiary hospital, to a globe sent by our Aunt Horror. On the globe our father clung to the deep South. He spun fast without flying off. When the globe slowed down, his head did a half-turn on his neck, then a turn back by half that. We tore the thing apart, duct-taped the entire planet, kicked it anywhere we wanted. Dented part of Asia, most of Antarctica. Had to re-tape.

Bender could see me. She looked at me, reading my ingredients. Hungry, we both had listened to the God-hype you had to swallow in order to be allowed to eat the soup at this mission. The tables were set in the chapel that once had a God's-eye skylight. Through the screen of sloppy black paint over the eye, full moonlight smudged her gaunt face and temples, her silvery upper lip and jaw.

She sang, *Hey now. Hey. That's what I feel.*

We were all sick to death from eating so much God venom. This serpent's voice tasted good. Her drumming bowed us lower over our bowls, our spoons witching the broth.

When she turned nine, Bender and I duct-taped her birthday cake—the wrong flavor and no icing—taped the candles, taped our cousin's bicycle handles, seat, tires, chrome fenders, who said he was forced to come to the birthday party.

We duct-taped our stepmother Dillo's hands to her knees because she napped curled up drunk, which was not birthday-appropriate we felt. For her convenience, we taped her whipping switch to her right claw. On another great occasion she had made us repair the broken switch, which we did, taping and overtaping.

Bender's voice scraped her own clogged reed:

Hey now. Hey. That's what I feel. How about you?

Of all hours, Bender should bless ours. Of all hungers she should solve them here.

You feel it? You feel it. You feel it too.

Our congregation lightly hammered our tables in tune with her coffin-lid-thumping boot.

Sixty-one years earlier, our mother told me nothing and no one could save my sister, that some darkness sings only darkness.

29

You never ask me about me, Bender said.

O Bender, I answered my sister-sawyer who had only survived her own self-killings because she sang.

You never ask me about me, she said again, though she knew I was afraid to hear her answer.

When she laughed she sounded forgiving.

Need duct tape? she asked.

I had become a musician along my way. I injured and reinjured my guitar until we both were near dead. Kicked out of the band, I marked it SOLD but kept it, slept with it, dreamed there was room for me in its shell.

I did. I needed some.

The thing—the foot ruler thing—in the shoe store—it tells your size? I can't remember what it is called. What is it called?

My feet were hurting, which caused me to try to remember what the foot thing is called. And I remembered, forgot, remembered. And then your gift for me arrived. The holiday scene on the tin container. The winter sky on the lid, the bowed heads of the horses, the two muffled drivers in the black sled. Scary. How much like the tin Vermont is Vermont? Out there it must be easy to open something so tightly sealed. And here, well, living is so easy they call it Assisted Living. Thank you for sending the Christmas cookies, which are ginger, a favorite. For future reference: ginger triggers my asthma. I'm happy to know that machines, too, make good cookies. I am amazed how alike the cookies are. That sounds like I am so damn old. Damn. I am. And I forget and then remember and forget it is a world in which a person can go to his computer window and look through and see what to have a so-called mom-and-pop company send to a hungry person. Send more, my dear son.

Is it called a Foot Measure?

I was watching the movie, edited

I was watching the movie, edited, of my once-wife, 4 minutes of her at 34, our sons 4 & 6—their pumpkin patch harvest of 1 dear pumpkin. I brought caramel corn, store-bought, for her and her new husband.

We were in the home of the younger, the older was there as well. My wife of 5 years was not there because the 2 grown men, 30 & 32 now, my merciless sons, refused to meet her.

New Guy was a good-natured person, a generous man and sensitive, and I could keep listing abstractions since he was an abstraction to me, but I will not. I was happy for the person who loved me real for 2 blessed decades and for a decade in the almost. Truthfully, I failed us more than she failed us. I was happy that she loved this good man, that he loved her with the-real-thing love.

He was trying to help in making all of this less strange for me. From love for him, she was trying, too. I was alone with them and our sons (his now), the movie ending fast. She rested her head easily and naturally against his chest, and he liked that, and the 2 men liked it, and the 4 drew closer who had no intention of excluding me in any way from their family.

They were not a family 3 decades old, a fact that mattered only to me. It was good for them that they were a fresh family who liked the movie, a fine family home movie with me nowhere in it, though I, strange guest, had been everywhere in it. It is good that their family decided that the mother, who did not have an affair like mine, was blameless altogether. Everything was best that way, is best that way.

I hope the story will always be kept so simple. I hope the 2 grandchildren will see the movie, which had once been an 8-minute film. They will ask New Guy and Grandma and Father and Uncle why. They will be told. And, alone in their room that night, I hope the older will ask, "What was he like?" and I hope the younger will ask, "What was he like?"

A pumpkin harvest like that one. 2 sons that were mine. 4 minutes edited out in which I was there like a father and husband.

We watched it 4 times, with little breaks between viewings.

Ladies Room

Len had spent eleven years cleaning the Mens rooms and the Ladies rooms in Mr. Prudowsky's three Asheville bars. Fine, private places. Marvelous venues for live music. Uncanny acoustics. A lucky job. But time to retire.

As he knew they would, the three ghosts appeared again in the Ladies Room of The Pea Vine at 4:30 AM, the middle of his shift. It was May 7, his ninetieth birthday. Len's checklist of tasks more or less done, he listened in.

They didn't know he was there in their afterlife as they rehearsed the same song, the one song. Between takes they talked about their husbands because, after all, they were not done with them.

They did not talk about Len. He knew he did not qualify. He was neither man nor woman to them. He had been a kind of motherfather to the band they had formed that called itself "Lula Town" after Millie's favorite Charley Patton song, "Mind Reader Blues." Millie, Dee, and Felice were musicians then, forty-some years ago, but they were in the nest and not yet flying.

He and his students had been music to each other: that flawed music with sweetness—and love—arriving in its flaws. His best students always outgrew him. Len was surprised how he missed them, missed their jarring phrasing, their improbable leaps to falsetto or gravelly inarticulateness or a full-octave skid.

"Let's find the head," said Felice to Dee. Felice, who was the lead vocal and also the rhythm guitar, had a thing about hating a stumbling start to a song.

Half an hour earlier, Millie had been the first to wind the spring of the talk about their husbands' crying. "He would blubber over some lake or river he remembered," she said.

And now she added, "Raisins. Raisins a special way in his oatmeal would make him cry. Or an untied shoe. Or steam on the window. You know: over the sink or in a store front."

Millie had no grip on the dobrojo's neck, so it simply hung, too high, on its strap. She should lower that. Len had told her many times.

Millie said, "You hear that?"

"Yep," said Dee.

Felice tightened the seat of the microphone. She asked, "Rain?"

There was no mike on Millie or on Dee. Millie's wooden stool was under the metal frame of a john door, and she had strung a wooden cowbell up. She liked to make a calucking sound with it for no good reason. Whenever she did, Dee hit the start button on the DryHands machine behind them. Millie said, "If he saw somebody tear up. Well. It's like somebody wet and gooey would make him—you know: wet and gooey."

Dee said, "Yep. It's like a crybabyman doesn't see it coming—and next thing happens is his noseholes are wet and he's dribbling like mine—"

"—mine mightcould fight the bawling—and not too good—or he might hide himself and lose it on the stairs or somewhere in the house, and you could hear him—"

"—he'd make that garbage-disposal sound in his throat and try to turn it off, really try—and mine said, 'Shit Dee, shit, I'm sorry' if he was crying—and he'd go right on with it and make a leaky, gummy mess of himself and not pull it together and—"

"They keep things," Millie said.

"—and—yes they do," Dee said. "Mine did."

Determined to bring them back to the music, Felice strummed a chord combination to remind them. It was always that C, F, G-minor at 4:30 AM in the Ladies Room.

Len had not imagined that common triad in the great beyond. He had pictured shadowed forests of staves, singing birds there: splendor. It was better than what he had pictured. And Millie's central role in the band: that seemed impossible. Like Len, she had an abnormally acute sense of pitch and rhythmic flow. She was utterly tireless in her commitment to music—like him. Like Len, she over-thought, and that meant she rarely got in her teeth what her talons captured.

At a rehearsal six years ago in the Ladies Room, Felice asked why Millie was missing.

"She's dead," said Dee. (Len wanted to ask, But—how is that possible?) Exasperated, Felice asked, "Again?" It apparently happened all the time. Dead. And dead again. Millie would miss two or three more rehearsals. Offering no explanation for re-expiring, she would return. She was a better musician each time.

He sat on an upended trashcan. He tapped his foot on tempo. He wished they heard him. He wished that they could vaguely make out the sight or the sound of him, as they had done when they took their music lessons from him.

Their hair and manner of dress changed on The Lethe Tour; their tone of voice and the key of their emotions shifted, though the conversation was always about their husbands' crying.

And it was always about the band solving the problem of the unwrapping part, of breaking open the first words of the old standard without Felice sounding like she had just hammered her thumb.

Len could not pull himself away because he had felt called there. He was there as he had been there for fifty-nine years, teaching many hundreds of musicians. Most gave up and became listeners, ashamed to be listeners, oblivious to how that mattered in their capacity for loving and being loved. Some developed into professionals; others, entertainers; a few, teachers. The failures, the most grotesquely bitter and resentful of the lot, insisted it was impossible for one person to teach another to be a musician; their graves were more spacious than their lives.

Learners had sought Len, had asked him to bring them inside the leaving-trail and the returning-trace of their own music. Though they had the humility to be guided, they taught themselves. That autonomy meant that at the right place of crossing, they dropped him for better guides, kept the connection with him, but barely recalled the depth of it.

It hurt him. It was all wrong. On certain mornings, however, when their music was pure sorcery, it was all right.

And this early May morning he knew what the terms would have to be if these three and his other twenty-six deceased students were going to actually see him; that is, if he was going to celebrate his ninetieth with them, and no longer be the invisible listener.

"How do we want it?" asked Dee.

Felice said, "We need a tickler chord or something."

Felice nodded at Millie, who glided over the bottom of C. It didn't work. She clawed a barred F. No. No.

Millie's dobrojo had come from a garage sale in Oteen, a town nearby. Len remembered her showing the inbred banjo/dobro to the band, telling them her whole life had changed. She could not have lifted her own newborn before her with greater excitement. It had been an important day for them all.

Dee said, "Here," and offered a tickler chord. She had learned before the others how to begin in the calm. She had mastered it in only a few lessons, and the others had learned it from her and then asked Len for the fine adjustments.

She was the first to forget it and to cause them to forget. Like all bands, Lula Town sent sparks flying, and put out its own fire. The nature of the beast.

"Mine had the trembly problem the last years." Dee strummed the top end of the G-minor on her guitar, a blond Gibson ES-335. (She had named it "Peetie Wheatstraw.") "I think we want something like this," she said.

Millie struck the cowbell. Caluckacaluckaluck.

You, he thought. Len knew her so well. If she eternally returned,

37

why did he feel such sadness about her repeated deaths? Because teaching was ordinary lesson-giving. Because it was the intercourse of learning. She had once let him draw a chord diagram on her palm in blue ink; when he apologized, he had used the word, "inappropriate," and she had said, "Beautifully."

"Something like this?" asked Dee, who started up the DryHands. For thirteen-and-a-half bars, it breathed into the room. No one laughed. At just the right moment during it, Dee firmly, calmly sounded a turnaround chord.

Every night of their appearance in The Ladies Room that moment repeated itself. The rest of their performance might change, but not that. Len had taught Dee the letting go of herself; she had discovered entirely on her own how to be a prankster in her improvisational playfulness.

The letting-go sounds were the ways to go in farther. Whenever he had taught this, Len called to mind a lifelong friend who had been in a terrible incident involving a Schwan's delivery truck, and had lost a hand and, later, a leg. "After the amputations," his friend told him, "you go in farther. Listen to this," he said, and sang "I'll Fly Away" in order to show Len he could sing better now that he could not play.

Millie said, "Do that again," and Dee dialed down the reverb, and strummed Peetie Wheatstraw, whom she sometimes called The Devil's Son-in-Law, The High Sheriff from Hell. Millie nested an easy coin-spilling arpeggio inside Dee's chord. "Give it," said Millie.

Dee gave it again. It was not the one.

"Are we waking up this song," asked Felice, "or putting it to sleep?"

Millie said, "Do that again," and Dee obliged, and Millie subtracted something that had only been ornamental. The sound was now more forlorn.

"Heard about Etta James dying last week?" Dee asked.

"Bad news for them," said Felice. "Good for us."

Millie said, "I cried when I heard it."

"Me too. Never cried the same in all the living time. Never once." Felice tapped the mike with her fingernail. The ice-splash sound stayed in the room. Len's temples and his toes and fingers were chilled by it.

Almost inaudibly, Millie asked, "Ever cry about Leonard?"

"No," said Dee, still making up her mind. "Yes," said Felice, undecided. "No," said Dee. "No," said Felice. "Yes," said Dee.

"Huh?" said Millie.

"It was time to quit him, learn from somebody better. I could've cried," Felice said. "I almost cried telling him."

"I told him all wrong—" Dee said. "I said, 'Leonard, you've gone as far as you go—and—I have to go on'—and I kept the tears. And inside me I cried hard."

Millie said, "I never cried for Leonard. Didn't cry when my husband died or my mother or father. Couldn't feel bad enough for myself about my own deaths to cry. But telling Leonard about moving on from him. Oh. I almost cried."

Felice tapped the mike again. Out came the sounds of the lower realms. They drew him in.

They drew him down.

His end was that simple. Len had heard the leaking sounds of his heart clearer every day of his life. Now, those train-whistles traveled away, whispering, falling quiet.

Felice breathed into it: *Don't know . . .* She tried again: *Don't knowww . . .*

"Isn't today the day?" asked Dee.

Millie said, "Yes. Yes it is."

"We were fishing before mine died," Dee said, "—and we had a camp in the woods at a little pool on Pigeon Fork but it was too *cold*

39

for fishing, and it must've been October—misty—like in October—and pretty leaves so bright you could see them right through the mist."

"Oh, Dee," said Millie, who had let in—and farther in—the sound of the word *Don't*. Far inside it, she was the Millie with no bar dividing the measure. And Len had been a—what had he been to her?

"Oh you," said Dee to Millie.

"And *you*," said Dee to Felice who was looking right through her.

Millie said, "They puddle up." Her sigh verged into pity and into pleasure.

"You see something?" Dee asked Felice.

"*You* see something?" Dee asked Millie who looked around the Ladies Room, looked right at Len, and didn't see him. Not yet.

"*Dee. Millie.*" Felice hummed the first three notes. She did not push hard, though she did push.

Dee said, "And some of the leaves were falling but I mean down-over-on-and-around us. And the top of his pole was shaking—and his cork was bobbing—

"—and he started leaking like he'd never stop."

Millie said, "Men puddle up. Something they can't do or won't is what sets them off. Or if they never could do something or something never would come to them and can't."

Millie had a feeling. She glided again over C. "You know, like calling to say 'You alive? Want to go eat something?' They can't do it. Can't help but cry about it."

Felice asked Dee if she could bring it; she meant: could she bring the calm again? Dee answered, "And I said to mine, 'Well, all your crying—it's funny more than it's sad, my dear.'"

Millie played the pulling-under tickler chord. The sound was respirable. It lived inside the instrument. It lived outside. It dissolved.

Dee played a quiet cresting wave. In perfect tranquility, Felice went far in: *Don't know why—there's no sun up in the sky—*

40

"And he said, 'Yeah' but cried harder a lot longer, and his mouth was trembly and his chin was already all wet—and by November he died, so that was as much answer as he was going to give."

Veterans Day

On Veterans Day, with no idea why, here we are snow-golfing
again in our usual threesome, exhausted, cursing, cold. Deadbeat,
widowed, divorced, we should be with our living parents at the Y,
the hospice, the home, but this is our place to do, die, be, at least
for now.

From driven women we have learned our names, and have had
practice in driving ourselves together, alone, and alone together
off the driving range. From driven men we have had lessons in the
poetry of the game. From our mothers we have been warned that
with our precise swing, back swing, and follow-through we were
perfecting nothing except becoming willing to dress and act and
take a mulligan and stroke our balls again and once again like
golfers will do on a freezing fresh-snow day like this, which is not
a fair day to golf, not an easy day to like, even in the good and
terrible linked company of friends.

On the third hole, I tee up and say, "Boys—when this snow
thaws—out come the sated worms—out come the sweet odors—
from the maze of tunnels—under the shallow—roots of the
ocotillos—

and mesquites and acacias—at the edges of all—this greenness—
and out come the burrowing owls squinting—at their young
ones—in the melting brightness."

My ball has curved away to the right over the rough and onto the
ninth green three fairways away.

Are my friends happy for me? They are.

"Eagletime," says Dwight.

"Like Elvis Muddy Wadsworth Tennyson," says Harry who blows
his hands and Dwight's concentration at the same time.

"All sky," says our prose poet, Dwight, after his three wood sends
the ball high, high, directly overhead and lands it almost on the
icy divot where it was teed. "All sky. All loss. All smoke spent in
holes where I went nowhere for twenty years with one woman
who gave me one kind of violent kindness when I most needed
to have none. One week of peace. One fucking week would have
been enough. One."

"Is this golfing—or what?" I ask.

Harry says, "Putt in the sand!"

Dwight says, "Long putt in!"

Harry asks, "My turn?" He shrugs snow off his arms, cants his
hips down, takes two practice swipes according to tradition and
his individual talent, and in an orator's stance he addresses the
ball: "I know you—don't I know you?—after all these years of
eating air from the mirrors in your empty bowls? What did you
admit to when I admitted everything to you? What hunger of
mine satisfied your hunger best? If I said it was too late to bring
my shame out of hiding, how would that strike you?" His line
drive smacks the door of a porta-john and ricochets back to him.

"We should have at least worn jackets," Harry says.
"Snow," says Dwight. "Driving snow."

43

"Who knew?" I say.

More or less, all three of us are regular men. We are Romantic,
Confessional, Counterfeit-Beat duffers in our middle, old, older
ages, slumped under the weight of our clubs which are the same
bag of bad choices and memorized verses we have lugged over
groomed paths and roughs and greens since our fathers in their
ultramarine Sansabelt slacks and matching phosphorescent green
socks and shirts first brought us. We didn't ask to be taught this
crass and subtle art exercised on military bases with military
passes for the civilian sons of veterans. We didn't ask then, we
didn't, but we still imagine our skinny arms round the griefs of
our middle-class clubhouse sages who believed
we believed in the poetry of cutworms and roses, of one kind of
beauty chewing another kind apart, who thought we thought this
mattered, this veteran's perk, this stylized sport of the set who
bought their memberships with their lives.

We were their Baby Boom troops tripped from our cribs and
whipped into shape by their words to the wise and those game
legs and war-sacked eyes. They cuffed us with their blunt leather-
gloved hands and called us by manly nicknames: Soldier, Buddy,
Bud, Guy, Man. This was the boot camp where they taught us
debarking, mapping, bivouacking, and laughing, belly-laughing
at ourselves and not by ourselves.

It was swell. We watched them laughing and we heard them
cursing, cursing at the flag and the club and the course ahead.
They fed us Cokes and bought us beer nuts and goofy gold caps,
and they drilled us and dragged us out against our wills for
another punishing nine

44

pilgrimages, nine lessons in leaning into, swinging through, lining up, reading the course, the green, the good lie, and lying good on our score cards with our standard-issue dull stubby pencils. They licked the tip and wrote, and let us lick and mix our spit with theirs.

It's a crime and a crying shame the way we visit the dead but never their graves. Even on Veterans Day. Our shoes crush pecan shells under the dust of snow on the steep path to the fifth hole set high above the long fairway's two berms and the three bare cloud-willows crowding the apron of the green.

"You first," says Harry who gives me the honors as the worst of us in this poetry. "Tighten your grip this time," says Dwight who has lost so much from tightening his so well.

"When this thaws," I say, "what races into—the dark pitchers underground are—sweet goodnesses only—that the locoweed and spiderling—and thistleseed can find.—The meek inherit— meekness, and the wind—pitches the meanest—of us into darkness—where we drink first and—outlast all grace."

Where I want to be I am. Where I want to be I am.

"Good lie," says Dwight.
Harry blows on his hands, says, "Mmmm."

"I am *teeing*," says Dwight. He is a constant man in all his wordloves. He practice-swings once and is ready. "No forms, rings, files, rungs, no gripes, no fake unforgivable grins and asshole canned lines, no loads, lows, lifts, no falling down,

45

climbing out of leaning into leaving from, no death, no burial,
no tomb."

The ball has sharply sliced off into nowhere.

"You'll never find it," I say.

Harry says, "Not a prayer."

"Want another shot?" I ask.

He does not.

Harry asks, "Sure?" but he is already teeing up, already shanking
his own shot into the thick cactus and mesquite some people call
The Rough, some The Jungle, and some The Shit.

Harry says, "I can't say it—what I miss most. Last vow? Last
curse? Cursing? Vowing? Warring? Being cursed? Our dead-end
anniversaries blessed by everyone who knew us? Our thirst? Until
the thought of death parting us seemed sacred."

I ask Harry if he wants to fall out. He slams the wood into the
bag, draws his seven, heads toward The Dark, The Bitch, The
Pit, says, "Listen to *him*," the snide way his dad said the same
words to my dad or Dwight's in the days when we followed them
into The Crap, The Swamp, the Deep, and shrugged off our
complaints, said, "Hell no," "Sure as hell," "Like hell," who never
broke stride, who knew our orders, who never said never.

It was criminal how they loved us, the old flaying, choking,
flubbing guy's guys. And we knew they loved us if we only knew
it almost in one practice swing once—their arms on our arms and
hands over our sixth grade unscarred hands.

Teaching me to scan, my Dad told me, "Dogleft and bunker on
top and a trap and tough approach with a five-iron slap and a
backspin chip up and a long roll on where it breaks right-to-left
and down."

Dwight's Pop said, "Skyed that one. Right on the pin. Eagletime.
Lost in the sun. Shanked again. Long putt in."

Harry's taught him, "Ass in the drink! Butt in the sand! Big gun.
Magic wand. Goddamn wind! Drove one! Dropped one! Dicked
one! Bogieman! Dripped in."

You could not convince us that was not nearly love. We were
convinced. We are convinced.

I suppose I am supposed to say their wives and daughters are
owed an apology for being kept away from these nine green
islands all those years ago and since. I am supposed to not contest
custody of this, supposed to beg women banging the glass ceiling
to forgive our lusts, our beer guts, our business suits, our hairy
backs and butts and cracks we made and make them kiss to come
in under par. Or I am supposed to add blame to the blame we
good old boys already assign to the good old crew of dads.

To be that way I would need more time.

47

On the ninth green, the wind in his teeth, Harry asks, "What should I miss first? Last second kiss? Last long list of tasks? Asking? Being asked?" He misreads the break, the depth of snow, mistakes his strength, and misses. "I miss asking to be asked," he says. "The trapdoor of sleep. Noose of dream."

"That's your best?" I ask.

Dwight says, "You're finished?"

"Par," says Harry. Liar.

We owe our fathers an unrepayable debt for both our certainty and doubt. It seems whenever we remember them we are given back again every acute joy and chronic grief, each one we remember about everyone.

Harry holds the pin for Dwight so he can line up the shot and wipe his eyes and face on his shirt, and speak out. Wordless, Dwight putts in from twenty feet, crystals arcing off the golf ball burning a green line across the whiteness to the hole you would swear was widening and caving in and deepening before our eyes and then sipping, then drinking, then swallowing.

Dwight reaches in. "I miss her. I miss him. What I miss is honest ugliness as venomous as a snake tattoo the size of the left side of your chest. As shameful. As useless. As murderously permanent." Determined to not even try, I pick up, and agree to the penalty.

"Boys," I say, "the clouds are pitching more snow—over the raked sands—and the tilted greens—and striped fairways and—onto the stunned bull snakes—in the glistening—yucca spikes. It is blinding—the cursed cactus wrens—their wings struck—by the shrike's puzzling shadow—in the golden flakes."

Are we done?

We are exhausted. It is late. Cold. The flag on the ninth green luffs and snaps in the wind. Ghosts in the snowfall laugh, cough. Curse.

Dwight asks, "Can we stand another round?"

"I can go nine," says Harry.

I say, "Sounds good," and salute.

"This is the grip," they said, and gripped us. "This is the form," they said who formed us, and said, "These are the rules we learned from the men who ruled us." Told us women just didn't get this awful poetry and never would. Asked us, "Don't you understand?" and understood we never could.

November 22

One day a year, but only one, Smoothie and The Tailor talk about the past. They buy a Proto-burrito and a small Styrofoam cup of refried beans at Proto's Eateria, and they eat in the back of the bus. They talk about the news, about their paper sales, their regular customers—as much as they can remember. They talk about the look of the new automobiles inside and out. They sing together a little. The Tailor is Smoothie's oldest living friend.

For over twenty years Smoothie has been bundle captain on the Route 9 bus in Las Almas, New Mexico. He distributes the newspaper bundles to the street vendors, and he troubleshoots for them. He chooses new members of the team whenever that must be done.

His first full day on the job was November 22, 1983.

The fare machine tumbled his fifty cents.

"Are you sitting here?" he asked the elderly woman, the sole passenger, because she had rustled mysteriously, had glanced at him in unsettling readiness as he sat down near her in the front of the bus.

"I'm always here," she answered. She removed her red vinyl shoulder bag from between them: the zipper closed around the nose of a gun barrel. "Bee. Two e's," she said. Her chipped nails were painted pale-sky blue. Her shining lipstick was Vaseline. Her damp hand went inside his, weakly gummed and gripped him.

"Where to?" he asked. He actually wanted to know. He wished he had asked differently.

"Going to hell," she said. "You going?"

One: where she was. Two: who she was. Three: where she was going. Four: what she wanted to know. In thirty seconds she had told him all of that.

The blackening sunspots under her eyes and on her temples were not at all attractive. Her short silver hair and her small ears were severely compressed against her head by a scarf. Her black eyes were gold-flecked.

Old leopard are the words that came to his mind. Later, he would write them down. He was a man who wrote things down. Long after, not knowing how they mattered, he would throw them away.

As the bus departed from the Mesilla Valley Mall, the doors made the hydraulic sound he liked on buses, probably because he had that sound in his memory, and it reminded him of how many years he had ignored public transportation. He had owned a car and known people who owned cars. He had rented a house when he had a job, when he was in circulation, had friends and still made new ones.

Bee said, as if to the bus driver, "Lord, look at him," and he was on the bus alone with her, so he looked at himself reflected in the opposite window. He should rinse his neck and face in a sink. He should slap the dust out of his black jeans, get a belt or rope to hold them up better. He should, he thought, recite the verses of his colorful t-shirt: that would—it always did—make him happy.

Heart-Healthy Nutritious
Supreme Smoothie!
Mineral-Infused Vitamin-Maximized
Supreme Smoothie!
Mouth-Watering Invigorating
Supreme Smoothie!

Out the window beyond them was more of the radiating New Mexico desert heat, the white match-head of afternoon light during the day and the icy wind at night. At Lenox & Elks, a stooped old man boarded, sweatshirt on and hood drawn close around his face. "Firey!" the old man said to Bee who said, "No lie," and said also, "This here's Smoothie, our new Captain."

Now Bee grinned, and the old man bent down to get a close look, and spit-laughed a stinking spray directly at Smoothie. Smoothie thought

51

it must have been that he was funny, that something about him was humorous. He said, "Do you always ride this bus?"

The man's face retreated a little into his hood. "The bundle bus. Bee's bus," he muttered.

Bee said, "Show Smoothie some respect,"

Talking through Bee to Smoothie, the bent man said, "Him? He's our new Bundle Captain?"

Smoothie said, "I don't—"

Bee said, "He—"

"Today?" the man asked.

"Today," she said.

Smoothie knew he could not add to or improve upon this kind of conversation. Once, it would have made him anxious to be talked about or at. In order to be rid of that, at thirty-eight he had been prescribed an anti-anxiety drug. The drug worked so well he was able to tell the unwelcome truth to his family members, to old and new friends at the newspaper production offices where he worked. He found that all of them thought he was a good man right up until the time he was actually an honest man. The drug released him from trying so hard to free others from their curses. It made him turn himself in for his own crimes. It made him run at blind cliffs of self-recognition. When he owed, he knew how much. When he fell, he saw how far. The drug was The Supreme Smoothie. It had taken only three years to sail him from what felt like the center of things to an unassignable destination.

Bee said that they were right on time for a call from The Super. When they pulled over at Telshor & Del Rey and stopped in front of the Shell, the pay phone was ringing, and she made him come with her to take the call.

She stretched the steel phone cable so she could stand in a wedge of shade from the building. She listened, she listened more, she pushed at the nylon shroud of her scarf and scarf knot; she said back to The Super on the other end of the phone line: "*I* name the day."

The black shade seemed to have bowed her upper body towards the ground. She cupped the phone to her ear, her other hand to the other ear. Smoothie thought he saw her cower. "Smoothie is his name," she said into the phone, and, "Well, you will soon enough." She handed Smoothie the phone. "Say hi."

"Hi," said Smoothie. "Route 9," said the other person in a tin-bell voice, "a good route."

Bee took the phone back. She stepped into the light, the silver phone cable and the handset glinting. She hung up, and they returned to the bus. He remembered his mother's voice, so much like the voice of Bee's boss. She had been the last of Smoothie's living relatives to die.

A woman in a knee-length paper-thin dress boarded, carrying a water-filled gallon and a cardboard sign. U Buy I Sing U Don't I Sing.

The bus made the steaming sound.

Bee, who knew her of course, introduced him as Smoothie.

Her sign facedown in her lap, the woman asked, "Is that name the truth?"

Smoothie said she could count on it.

She greeted the old man as "Tailor," and took the seat next to him, offered him her gallon. She had to punch his arm to keep him from draining it.

"Give a crush," The Singer said to The Tailor who tightly grasped invisible oars as he puckered up, and they leaned toward one another in their small imaginary boat, and kissed so hard they slurped.

The Singer sang, not nearly loud enough. The Tailor and Bee sang softly with her, *All at once am I several . . .*

The bus driver probably sang, but in any case, some bass crept in. It could have been the bus driver.

When they were done and the bus was accelerating again, the group seemed to appreciate Bee's honest assessment of it as unjustifiable songicide. They applauded her, and Smoothie joined them. Bee opened her purse, raised it and swung it in front of her so that it seemed like a small puppet making a bow or curtsey for her. She sat.

"He'll do," said The Tailor.

"He might," said The Singer. "Starts tomorrow?"

Bee said, "That's the plan."

Smoothie could not fathom how Bee had chosen him. He looked the part; it was the opportune day; his need seemed the greatest: this is what he later speculated.

He was offered a handshake from The Tailor, and, from Bee a pat on the shoulder, and, from The Singer the gallon, which he refused. She unsuccessfully offered again. She rummaged in her dress pockets, stood up in order to rummage deeper. She hooked what she was fishing for but only fingered it, only looked into the pocket, without withdrawing her hand. "Got it," she said.

"Good," said Bee. "Little gift?"

The Tailor leaned forward, gave Bee the on-the-downbeat signal of people in a band.

The Singer offered Smoothie an unwrapped glycerine suppository in silver foil.

The object mattered to her. Its bubble was triple-coated in space-age plastic; its crenellated foil backing was embossed, compounding its mystery and communicating its worth with a holy invocation: **EASYGLIDE**. Smoothie could see how it mattered. It was cool to the touch, and it smelled of warm silverware drawn from a soapy sink.

He accepted.

It was time to accept.

54

Now The Tailor asked, "How long?"

"Hard to say," Smoothie answered. He held the silver-cloaked bullet up to the light. *How long have I been homeless?* he thought. It had all begun three years ago; he had landed on the streets two months ago, or weeks, or even less. He decided he wouldn't answer The Tailor until he could remember.

"It found me," said The Singer. The gray tip of her tongue moistened her lower lip. "It did. It did." Smoothie could almost imagine the unlikely path; some teenage driver would think how funny the suppository would be as payment for a newspaper; some doctor would offer it with confusing instructions.

Smoothie gave the suppository back, for which she was grateful. It could have traveled to her from galaxies eons away. She held the suppository package near her face and read it with the desiccated bark of her fingertips, her transfiguring strangeness emerging into full view.

At the Flea Market stop Temp and Tech, dark-skinned twin brothers, Smoothie's age or a little younger, or fifties, or late fifties, introduced themselves.

Tech and Temp were found in the Valley View Elementary dumpster, dead from exposure, on December 7, 2001. In 1989 The Singer's daughter boarded the bus, told them The Singer had died two days earlier on September 11, from undiagnosed cancer. They had never met her, though they knew of her. She asked for a crush. Her voice, familiar to them all, verged on song. She got off at Telshor & Del Rey. The driver, at sixty-three years of age, died of stroke on the Route 9, at Roadrunner & Foothills, Veterans Day of 2000: a lasting sleep after a drive-thru meal at Proto's. Bee took her own life on November 22, 1983.

Tech and Temp carried twelve newspaper bundles on board. They sat atop the two high piles like Rumpelstiltskins.

"Our new Bundle Captain," said Bee.

"He's ugly, ain't he?" said Tech.

"Correct," said Temp.

Tech and Temp received a crush from The Singer, and she forgot herself and gave them another, forgot herself and gave another, longer, to The Tailor. And then there was soft off-key singing, *Can you hear a lark,* and everyone, including Smoothie, singing, *in any other part of town?* And The Singer, fanning herself with her signage, grinned at him.

And Tech said, "Loverly," and Temp said, "Es verdad."

Inside him, Smoothie braked. His thoughts pedaled backward—better at that than moving forward—and he counted the crew members: Tech, Temp, The Singer, The Tailor, Bee, the driver, and himself.

His first day on the Route 9 bus. His first day as bundle captain. He asked, "What day is it?"

The bus stopped at Mesa Grande & US 70. A woman with an almost-newborn, those tiny hands reaching out of blankets, stepped up into the bus, glanced at all of them. She stepped off.

Smoothie thought the baby in those rosy blankets had sounded like it might say something. It didn't have words, but it had emitted a wordsome gurgle. The Tailor looked like 2 AM and The Singer a little before. The brothers, perched side by side atop their bundles, stretched out their legs next to each other, like clock hands in the minute-past-midnight position. Their worn khaki pants were the same country club color of marigolds.

"What day is it?" he asked. His first hour ever completely surrounded by the crew. He asked them all, "What day? Tell me." He was too embarrassed to ask what year, what month.

"Eighty-three—November twenty-two," said The Singer as if that was an answer. Her face was crusted with sunspots at her temples and jaws, the same as Bee, as The Tailor, Tech and Temp. The brothers had swept-back white hair and very full identical fu manchus; they breathed through their blistered mouths, blowing yellowing white moustache hair outward.

Smoothie stared because he wanted to stare. On his meds he acted and, in fact, *was* like the human a human might think he was. He stared at their lean jaws and slack, squamous necks and heads, and at the unlit jewels of their eyes.

They stared back, baring what teeth they had left. He said, "You call *me* ugly?"

"We agree on it," said Tech. Temp nodded, with conviction.

Bee said, "You really are. But—"

Temp said, "Plain fact."

"Homely," said The Singer.

The Tailor said, "All your life, I bet," and seemed to size up Smoothie for a custom ugly suit.

The driver raised his hand, though he had no question. He was pointing at the sign above the windshield: DO NOT TALK TO THE DRIVER WHILE THE BUS IS IN MOTION.

Bee said, "Unanimity," evidently pleased that her crew could be so accurate about Smoothie. Smoothie remembered a half an hour earlier when she had handled her purse that certain ventriloquist way.

"He's 'homely,' then," said Tech. "We agree?"

Definitely. The driver might have said it, Smoothie couldn't be sure.

The driver had stopped the bus at Roadrunner & Morningstar where no one came on, but where the fare tumbler loudly chewed coins, and the inadequate engine hmmphed and huffed under the bus hood.

The doors steamed shut and the STOP sign near the driver retracted like a wing stump or a gill. When the driver's shrill-sounding wide turn emptied all the brightest light from the bus, Smoothie asked, "Will you tell me what time it is?"

"No," said the driver. It was him. Or it could have been him.

Bee told The Singer to fan Smoothie, though he doubted if she meant for her to fan so hard, circulating the diesel and gasoline exhaust that perfumed them all.

Smoothie said, "Put that down. And don't look that way at me: I don't want a—" he caught the switch in her expression—"crush. And —" she was already humming—"no song, okay?" Already, the words were coming, *"Are there lilac trees—"*

"Is that your whole damn repertoire?" Smoothie asked.

A man, unnaturally tall, a spotty thin gray beard furring his chin and neck down to the bottom of his throat, leaned over Smoothie. He had come from nowhere. His shaved head was shiny and smelled of oranges studded with cloves. He kissed Smoothie's forehead. "Plenty of time. S'early." He did not move. Smoothie could pull away but. Smoothie could wisecrack, he could be rude, but.

The man said, "S'almost one in the afternoon, Captain." As if Smoothie had been awoken from a pirate nap, his head still far inside his pillow, his closed hands warm under it. As if a dream had placed him on a bus with steam sounds, with a motor coughing and coins clinking and his mother's singing voice fading.

The gray man had been the last on, but he was the first dropped off with his bundle of newspapers at the westernmost part of town, the stop at Roadrunner & Morningstar. Smoothie thought he heard Bee say, "No one will pick you up at 7:10," but he misheard.

Later that evening—promptly at 7:10—everyone on the bus called out to him, "Grayman!" He boarded.

Grayman was fifty-one. He was as old as he would ever be.

He took Smoothie's elbows into his hands. He took Smoothie's forearms, firmly took them, pulling him forward. Grayman's ears and eyelids and brows and temples were sunburned almost black. For the longest time, he did not let go.

At 6:50, before they picked up Grayman, they picked up Tech and Temp at the Flea Market. Tech reported that he and Temp had sold almost fifty. He reported it to Smoothie. Smoothie, flustered, said, "Well. *Well.*"

"God *bless*," muttered Tech.

Before them, at Lenox & Elks, The Singer boarded. "Poor sales," Bee said, not quite loud enough to be heard. "Always, poor sales." Bee nodded at the facedown sign. "The singing hurts sales."

The Singer shared the water bottle and good crushes all around. At 6:40.

Before her, The Tailor—"Good location," said Bee, "Telshor & Del Rey"—climbed aboard at 6:30. He jingled his change-maker and held up his coin-stained wooly palms, and everyone high-fived him, Smoothie and Bee last.

Bee and Smoothie had spent the day at what was his new, his destined location, Lohman & Telshor, where she showed him the ropes as she had been shown by her predecessor.

Hardly believing where he was now, Smoothie wondered where he was then.

On that same day in '63, he was nineteen years old and at a job interview for copy reader at the *Las Almas Sun-Times.*

The interviewer, a very old man, shoulders bowed, back bent, had him sit down. He waited for the young man to settle before telling him the news about The President. He explained he had over forty years in at the *Sun-Times.* It was done. It did no good to hope it wasn't. Drawing typed questions from a clean manila folder, the man then tried to interview Smoothie. At that time in his life, Smoothie had a name. For the life of him, he couldn't remember his full name: the answer to the first interview question. The old man's eyes and Smoothie's filled with tears. The two felt as if the bones and muscles and the skin of their faces could not hold. Tears poured into their throats.

"Impossible," said the interviewer, instantly not a stranger at all.

Smoothie tried. He could not speak.

He remembered thinking that the interviewer was right. To be flung from the world as if you were a word crossed through: impossible.

A word to Teacher Reptile's readers and their parents on the occasion of Father's Day and the anniversary of Teacher Reptile's release from Eight Gates Correctional Facility

Seekaaa. Seekaaa. Seekaaa!

Once before The End Time was a time Teacher Reptile had served His time. You could hear old woodpusher roll to visit children readers, parents, too, on His Vision longboard. Roll sick, old school, yo!

Seekaaa. Seekaaa! Seekaaa.

Said Teacher Reptile to parents all unrapturable, "Heard you be four down on Death. Heard harsh bail, no heaven. Here be I then, hurry or delay, here come I."

What can you do? You do not—naturally, you do not Teacher Reptile's noble visit on half-pipe want. What can you do? He be sent. He your child's Savior be.

One thing about prison, maximum vert, dear Children, dear Childbearers, crawling out—out of the hole after a face plant by 5-0—is that you own a wallet, but things in it are not money, pictures are not family, not anymore. You go looking first for cons you know snaked out, out before you, nut-shwankered, rattlers carved off, venom used up, who own cheesy cell phones—is that not funny?—*cell* phones—with their answering biff, Not here right now…have reached…sorry we missed…leave name, leave message, leave your, we will return your. Wha. Wha. Wha.

You, old cellmate, out Freshly Ground, you will be screened when you make that call, that's one thing—or Wife, Kids, Sammich, Grambich, Grampich might pick up. If this occurs, Teacher Reptile will say flat out, "I was old dad's cellmate." Anything else:

61

pointless. "I'm dad's old love muffler," "I'm taking a poll of fellow middle-age prison sex slaves"—say that, Teacher gets His phone hanged—Teacher Reptile!—a hanged phone! Imagine that. Not that He is or a slave was, you wouldn't take a poll, tell you what.

You could call Him a disc jackey. He scripted. He spinned. The Air He ollied. By The Radio Signal was He transmitted beasty. Shiznaz He endured, dear Childbearers, dear Childbeings. Old equipment lifted He. Bad music laying around the lair was taken, yes, Him Taker Criminal, Him Teacher Reptile, same are, same were.

Teacher murder threatened some, some Burt old mullet rats asking for asphalt hankie. Equipment disappeared. Musics, ever eezer, absent often around radio station were where said jackey served. Programming FM—twenty-one years' service— citizen solid, man model—murder threats aforementioned, some necessary irrecoverable injuring of said Burt mullet rats—therwise upstanding hesh woodpusher jackey on His manikgreen shaggin wagon—Seekaaa! Seekaaa. Seekaaa. Seekseekseek.

Some sletching you expect, some jacking long-term—am He correct? Am righteous Teacher right again? People act surprised by crime. She surprises she. Long hospital stay be butter snitches never anticipate actually.

Judges, lawyers, parole officers, reporters want remorse expressed.

Not here right now, not reached, not missed, not re-morse, not first morse.

Remorse Ancient Teacher Reptile possesses not.

You Children grown who be reading, reading along (include yourself, you little Jackinocchios, you Jackerellas), readspeedin or cutting muffins in your post-criminal daddy's or mommy's chudded-out laps, sidepipe in your PJs, of mad chill wallies dreamin, of stalefishgrab, He write for you.

He write for you. Teacher unrehabilitated might have been your future cellmate—worse if He be cellmate past. Then He bephone you, make you wonder how did He get your number, *how*, bephoning over, planning to visit unwelcomed!

Seekseekaaaseekaaaseeka! comes Teacher. Word.

Shitshit, say adult parent convicts-ex, no I never mentioned that I knew Teacher, no I didn't think He could find us—He has!—His message said He wants a callback. He is not a changed man, He said He hasn't changed. I want a cellcall! said Teacher Reptile.

Teacher's fame has not Him changed—count—don't—on that. Just give er. Just give er, eh?

He be your sketchy episode of Ring of Lords, of War Stars epochal reprequels. He offer Wrath for Rapture Generation, Wrath for stick-kicking chestcheckers, Wrathflip for under-twelve bombsuicider P.O.S.E.R. in Wisconsin, Mississippi, Michigan, Florida, Ohio, Kansas, in Texas-Crawford.

Have His wak cell call your cheesy, shizell cell. Call His nom de plume, "Teacher Reptile," call Him Teacher, what future junior convictettes and convict graduates call Him.

Remorse is one Tweet optimum popsicle!

Ask Grambich, Grampich to get you some. They must His newest book purchase, newest just out, kewl beans, sixth *Wrath* book in fourteen years, *Wrath of Vert Ramp*, blurber Laura Bush Lady First Former, printings multiple, translations worldwide. American JK Rowling, noggled youth call Him. That He am, that He am, sixty-nine-year-old-born-again cicada, singing shibby, spooky insect-face-picture back of black-on-black embossed book jacket. Teacher look stellar, see how Him spawn of Silverstein Shel, Dahl Roald, Kafka Franz.

Poor you, your children prise Him from wine-red shelf at mothership chain. *This be one book I want!* They hug *Wrath* Volume Sixth to their obeez hearts, sludgehammering ameriyoung, part of the continuing series. They want new *Wrath*.

Picture that, picture it.

You thought—you hoped—your loved ones He might never meet? That He dissed easy be by you, famous too by far to care like this about you?

64

He be coming, coming BSLT, firecrackering your stairs.

Seekaaaseekaaa. Seekseekseek. Seekaaa.
Outside out, is it not? God rapturing only swass young. Rabbits with holes in, crocodiles with wooden legs dragging.

End time. God only wolfin young suffering unto broad golden Godapron.

Your virgin oogles thrill to meet Him, admit, admit. You be gone soon enough. End Time! End Time.

Accept.

Accept, at last. Teacher brings you something toobular, photo opportunity even, if you want, if they, if we.

You, after all, were there. Beginning of Teacher Reptile's career. Remember, dear hamburger toes, He started writing His *Wrath* books in stir, riding drafts griptaped. Stirring was He, young jedi! Asking questions all imprisoned ask: Yo, who define my sheise demographic?

So many, many prisons, so much slam privatized, so many prisoners' childrenamerican not reading Rowling, Tolkien, Milne, Berenstain, Lewis, Seuss, JRR, RD, JK, AA, CS.

You were there, dear cellmates, you were. You could tell Teacher was free-crawling, childway, finding, tasting extreme bliss tweakage, checkin midge, slammed, stapled, limboed, finally stuck it, He just jimmied, then He jimbo, He technical, He

T.B.C. In good time, in once upon, all in good time. He read aloud to you, Randall, John Crowe, John A., Dylan, Delmore, John B., Mark Van, Allen, the hardtime yardschool. His readers missing their fatherses, their absent grampiches, shitsnack Michaeljackson grambiches, hardyoung at heart, wanting more *Wrath* at first and at last from dependable Reptile supplier of Apocalypse.

Inside old school religion be young school. Guess which rabid reading *Wrath* to whom?

Ancient Teacher Reptile good for stories if you only leave Him snakeskins left by people still in prisons, leave Him deludings, presumings of innocence, scaly bibs and bibstraps offsloughed.

What He do is He put our snake back in your original skin, about ninety-thousand rough bookwords, three revisions to sleeve your thing. He was here, been here boardskating since Eden stoked from slime rose, was primo eel black, lost was, now arrives Happy Meal only for boardskaters in a fire gap. Lazarus having naked left tomb enters fearsome on page one.

Seekaaa. Seekaaa. Seekseekaaa. Skitchin on the Jesus train!

O, men! O, bards mortal in your amen circle at yardtime, your holy infants ask that more *Wrath* be toss from Teacher Reptile's pen. Make He tender your inhuman. Make He mild your silent ones bleeding. Mark He by spirit sign your beast baptizing.

Could you parents kingdom unbarred enter? Your children chosen, but you never?

Read me this but play it loud vile, Teacher once asked cellmate Manberry Dreamjohn. This passage must transport, say He, daily bread at holy hour break, sacred wine drink for your bookriding young. Done, our strangulations, Done, our knife heels biting. Wet blood of words on our cutting blocks.

New readers He ever need. Readers now be sinless young who trust, who trust, who witness trauma firsthand must—plus terror, if possible—second by final second must smell death's strong cologne weaponized in the grinding shadows Kiplingesque beyond pillows blankets bedsheets pressed just crisp. Justice do not teach remorse. Justices supremely teach it less, dear Crip in crib, dear Republicmother in can, reading this. This He—am He your true Reptile Teacher?

Life visiting after death consoling is whenever Department of Corrections returns a Corrected One. So come He to you a sixth time, in eternal volumes more. He that Am am not for thee but for thy children come, The Ancient Teacher Reptile, the Jamesking 21st century edition, sweet stellar, yo, the bringer of the wicked awesome.

Seekseek. Seekseekseekaaa. Seekaaa.

Seekaaa.

A glossary of terms for the Teacher Reptile tales appears on the last page of *57 Octaves Below Middle C.*

When will we speak of Jesus?

So you're The New Silence.   You're going to like the job: the
band kids, those kids are great, you're going to love
them   and how they love you no matter what, and the fans,
you're going to like them, and if all goes well they're going to
laugh at you— it's real cruel and real   connecting.
You're going to like all of the really, really good nothing that
comes with this job. As the retiring Silence I'm glad to offer
some thoughts. It used to be that I didn't manage transition, I
was transition-averse, and at a time like this in which I'd lost the
best job I ever had I would lose some reception, kind of like a TV
set.   I'm just not that way anymore, I don't lose reception, I'm
on day and night, I've got volume.   It's why I lost the job as
The Silence—well, you know that.   The band director asked
me to keep this email orientation short. I said I would
meet with you in person. He said NOT. I get that. I get that. I
do.   This first email will be a start anyway. It's the
right day for this— people would call it auspicious, which the
dictionary says has its root *in spicius*, which means *giving spit*. In
the papers today the print was smeary from rain, and it's the acid
rain that almost takes all the print right off, or it makes it smeary
and the headlines are all-of-a-sudden like mysteries: WOMAN
WITH FIVE BREASTS GIVES BIRTH TO ONE POPULAR
FOOD CHAIN RELEASES HOLDINGS   It's no wonder
people read their news online these days. Take the band kids—
the band kids hate newspapers. They'll tell you these things,
you don't have to ask. You fall in love with them because—
you fall in love with them plenty and for plenty of reasons, but
that's one. You've probably been told—I wonder have you been
told?—the idea of The Silence for Dominion High's marching
band was to do something good for laughs. The band was known
as the State Champion of Unfunny all those losing seasons.

The idea-less band director—that's not bitterness, me calling him
that   —well, yes it is, it is, yes—   he stole the idea from a
band in Corinthian, Texas, that had the idea but
took it too serious.   They needed the right job description,
the man who would match it. The band kids had to be in, had to
be down on the concept, the interview, the outfit, the layout of
the terms, the musical marriage. The bandgirls wanted Poetic.
The bandboys Pitiful.   You need to be awfully out of shape for
this job, extremely laughably out of shape, body and mind,
"ambulancable," the cymbalist said to me. Her lips are six-ring.
Six in her brows. Six in her ears. You'd have a problem finding
one bandface that's unpierced.   I'm sure somebody told you all
this when you applied, that you'll be a better Silence if you're a
White middle-age guy in worse and worsening shape. I'm not
being cute about this. It's true.   Here's what I want to say: bad
appearance is everything when you're out there on the field,
when the failure needs to be the full-failure—   "cardiacular" is
what one of the cornets called it. You seem to be the rubber knife
when you break the band's marching.   You seem to be the toy
drill when you're punctuating the band's dramatic pauses.
Everything just stops.   Full stop.   The full stop that's
unimaginable. The marching, the music, the directing,
everybody's in mid knee-raise, half-pivot, pre-blat,   pre-
blow, pre-trill. The marching rows don't collapse, but almost.
You're air-drumming, tubaing the air, air-batoning. And if you're
not   actually   the   actually the   saddest thing
on earth, you're not funny.   What I want to teach
you is that you're the real knife. You're the real drill.   In the
Graying Nation section of the paper an article today says—I'm
looking at it, I don't carry this stuff in my head because then I
lose it—   an article says memory dissolves more

69

rapidly in water-based entities than in soil-based entities. The article explains it was all discovered in a study of ancient permafrost pebbles—this is a crypto-science, it's a whole crypto-science called paramettafollogy, worldwide, growing, has an institute in the Aleutians.   The article says memory persists, they have found that it persists in the bowels of ornithoscrofa. An ancient boar creature. Memory persists in boarpebbles scientists call "UE," "Unforgetful Excretions." They're the shape and size of ocarinas or of   baby mittens. UE is the proof you have. It's what you have if you're a human scientist, which means   you're a water-based entity, I guess. If it was right between my sons and me, I would want to talk with them about this.   Or if it was right between my friend Abraham and me. I would.   Talk with him. Them.   I talk now, plenty. It's not like before. When I got the job as The Silence I had the talent. The uniform didn't fit, so it perfectly emphasized my beer gut, which had a side-to-side and up-down flap, had a happy snout, gave off glare, produced glow. I was junkfooding a lot—   it was right after I left my wife   and I was pretty naturally comically repugnant.   I was. I want to say this about the pants, that the pants are not everything like the director might tell you, but they matter, they should hurt, the fit should hurt, the pants have to be in The Sausage Style if you're The Silence. It's the job, that's all I'm saying is it's the job and when you start to fit it differently do something else. You get a clowny rayony skin-tight tubetop thing—all of it is in the Dominion band colors—and, well, you have your uniform by now—have they issued you that?— gold and green, white piping—   the tubetop hurts and the marching boots hurt and, like I said, the pants, but the cap is too big and is painless, and fortunately, that doesn't compensate.   It doesn't. My friend Abraham, blind, Ray-Bans, extra-long white cane, class act, fit, groomed, right in his mind, a formal fellow and religious since losing his sight, regular and pagan before that, a retired welder, says the arc was what did it.　　He　　was my friend, twenty-five years Abraham was my friend—　　now *there* was a man of *many* questions. For instance, when I told him the rain made everything smeary, that it worried me, and when I said, "I think this is funny, Abraham, listen to this headline, mysteriously funny, 'SWEETENING THOUGHT SAFE,'" he asked, "Has any single part of your heart survived?" He asked, "When will we talk of this?"　　After the divorce attorneys started guiding her and me through our own intestines, when I told Abraham I took the job as The Silence, told him, "Here's one, 'SENATE REJECTS PROTECTION FOR ENDANGERED KNOB DWELLERS,'" he asked, "Have you bought a bus ticket to hell?　　What have you done? Do you know what you've done?　　When, when will we talk of this?" A tree is　　maybe　both. A tree is probably　both water- and soil-based.　　A cat will get high up in it and forget something, like about climbing down or jumping.　　It will make that sound which is, which I want to say is watery, but that's not it, it's not the sound of that.　　It's the crying you make if you don't mean to but you're mocking the specialness of your own crying. It's forgetful about itself: *I'm crying, I'm not going to stop because I think I was a cat—I'm making cat sounds aren't I?*　　*I forget.*　　*I forget.*　　What if two cats get treed in the same tree at the same time?　Same thing? Half of it in the air, half of it in the dirt, a tree—I haven't exactly worked out this part—　is not as funny as the cat.　　This is instruction I'm offering.　　It's the kind of thing the band kids will help you better with.　　My first day on the job one said

71

to me, "Mr. S, your glasses have two lenses the same color. It just ain't funny." She brought me duct tape she had already bought— kid from a poor family—　　　 her piccolo a rental, her swollen, angry piercings, her whole sweet face the amateur's paradise— spent her money correcting me, taped one lens, broke and hypertaped my nose-rest.　　　 If you do good at this— tromboning, oboe-ing air, saxing, horning uninstrumented, you know all that part, of course—the band kids will boost you after the game. That boost, I don't know how you replace it when it's lost.　　 Don't blow them off, Mr. New-On-the-Job—listen to them. "Mr. S," one told me a week before the big Dominion vs. Adams game, "you wants you some pee stains." Good advice. I'm sharing it with you for free.　 "Release more butt crack," they told me, "Bare more man boob."　　　　　 Yours.　No charge. Self-injury does best. A beast of a hernia bandage. Foot in a monster cast.　　 If their parents tell them The Silence kicked ass, the kids'll tell you.　 I was a success because I got all of this: the nothingplaying, the nothingmaking: four full bars of soundless.　　　 And then there's the after-soundless full-band blast, of course, and you act terrified because you are, because that's it,　　　 that instant of you being the source of the stadium vacuum.　　　 And this is about the key point I want to make.　　　 It's the hatchet-severed head, it's the heart or the foot or the carved-off face floating in the splashing bucket of blood that makes gore-horror so good. And, afterwards— the kids taught me this　　　　 —so funny.　 People applaud you　 if you are a good Silence. People of all generations. They jump from their seats.　 Calls come from the local radio personality, the sports reporter from the paper, the yearbook kids.　 Pictures, yes.　 Preferably terrified-looking. Words, no. Words, never. You can tell I couldn't do that now.　　 Not

afraid enough.   Not silent.   My last day ever on the job, I
was in the men's room. I   —I was in the men's room,
wasn't I?   —It was after the big Dominion vs. Adams
game, and I was feeling good because one of the band kids told
me I was "so fuckupular."   The kind of kind thing the
kids would say to me.   I had successfully tried a maneuver the
kids had told me might be good for laughs during the terrifying
blasts.   They said blast-break might be a good time for a dick-
check.   They rehearsed me that: the left-hand high-thigh grip,
thumb-out two-lift, little shank torque, little shake-yank.
The bandboys said higher. The bandgirls said harder.   I
dialed that, did higher. Expert.   Redialed, did harder.   I made
it work. I made it work. I was so fuckupular.   I made
something out of what it all was.   When you leave like
that, when you leave a good person like I left my wife—a good
person outside and in—and you've left for thirty years' worth of
reasons—thirty honeying years thirty stinging—but you've also
left for love of another—and your two grown sons your lifeblood
your heart and your head—your two sons leave you totally—
totally and finally—because of you carrying on with the other—
because they forget everything but that—because they are just
humans—they might lose their jobs their lovers their friends—
might lose more all the time—and they loved you beyond
measure they loved you like mad but they forget they forget—
and because they're water-based you can't believe how they can
hate how they can hate and how the spill of their hate is
endless—   when you leave like that, the sound goes out
like something's gone wrong or terribly right with the set.
A show was on.   Of all the shows on your TV it was the
funniest because it was the saddest.   *First things pass first* is
what I want to say, unless, unless   what I mean is *First*

73

things pass, then true things pass.   Then truer.   Then the truest.
What happened was that the band kids had changed into their
street clothes, and they'd left me.   There.   The men's
room.   The men's room, I think.   I was feeling I had
triumphed. The dick-check had worked. It was scary.   Dick-
check scary. And I do not say that lightly.   I was lingering
there.   Somewhere.   The men's room. Not really wanting to
change clothes, not wanting to get dressed   I don't know
why   I don't unless I do   I guess I do— I didn't want to
get dressed because of my triumphant success, because before I
was The Silence my divorce news had torn out the tongues of
everyone around me.   That had been my solitary achievement.
And, then, on the day of the big game, I had gotten some help
with that, had known how to make something out of the horror
of it, of what that all was.   Touching and   not
touching   my face, I looked into the men's-room full-
length mirror, the stenciled black lettering on it demanding, DO
NOT TOUCH. DO NOT TOUCH. DO NOT TOUCH. I
was   obeying.   I was untouching, untouched.   That's
when Abraham caned himself in.   Tapped towards me,
and knocked and   tapped his metal cane-tip on the tile
floor between my feet.   And why was he there, why, since he'd
told me the day before that he didn't know me, didn't, thought
he had, it made him ashamed to have ever known me or believe
he did. Why was he there?   Together, we looked blindly at
the mirror. If your height was four-five, you'd call it "full-
length."   He knew me when I had sons, family, friends,
one job I did, one place I   lived, one way I saw me, the
same way he saw me.   He tapped and knocked my uniform
pants   at the cuffs,   at the knees.   He tapped my inseam.
Now here's something. Here's something in the paper that I

74

believe is notable: CINDY MCCAIN RESPONDS TO
GATES.   I told him. Abraham asked, "When?   When?
You and your demon: when will we speak of Jesus?"   That's
how I took the new job in Extraellaville. That's when I lost the
old job of The Silence. That's when the opening came up—that
you filled.   (You've got my email address.   I've got yours.
I like email.   You'll see: I can be helpful. I've just begun.)
I haven't seen Abraham, not since he asked his question.   His
question was what caused me to start talking and talking.
Wanting to say something. Wanting   to say what I could
have,   to hear, to be heard when I say what I want,   which
is nothing, I mean   —but that job is done,   it's done.
And I'm talking,   talking,   talking, talking,
talking.   And talking.   I talk and I talk too much, way
too much, I know.

          I'll shut up.   I'll shut up   eventually.   I will

All of the stones all at the same time

The client scratched at paste clotted in his hair.

The client was in a car. The client's car was in a car space between newly painted golden lines.

A sign: Mini Bob's Mart.

"We are quite lost," said Deer Food.

The client asked, "Isn't this Mini Bob's Mart?"

"Bob's Mini Mart," answered Deer Food.

"So." It was as the client thought: Mini Bob's Mart. He had learned that arguing with Deer Food was pointless. When a small matter could be disputed, Deer Food, the client's hallucination, would dispute.

Deer Food sucked in smoke, crushed his cigarette butt against a burn-scarred left paw pad. His teeth were stained, the fur around his mouth was nicotine-green, the fur at his paw-tip and brow was singed green. If the client concentrated upon all of Deer Food all at the same time there was more of Deer Food to concentrate upon. Deer Food's chin damp. Deer Food's tail pumping against seatback. Deer Food's breathing sounding like wiper-blades.

The disoriented client could not find his way home. The client did not know that he was three miles from his house, that he was two blocks from Dr. Guelderose Darshan's Neurobiofeedback Clinic. Dr. Darshan bald but for electric-white hair follicles, which the client at this time could not summon through concentration.

The client, parked at Mini Bob's, felt his brain struggle as it produced, half-produced, reproduced a phantom, his younger brother, his brother phantom he should recognize from memory: a form moving in him as if behind glass, a bowing and kneeling form very slowly shelving small items of great volume. The client, lost, did not recognize shelver, shelf, shelved, door, shop, car, car space. The client did not recognize the road from which he had pulled in, or the place he held in the world, or the world holding him. The client felt he must have once been in this place with his phantom, that his phantom had once held a job in a mart like Mini Bob's, that his phantom had moved there beyond him but had appeared before him. He felt he could have opened the door to Mini Bob's and said to his phantom, his brother, that he would be there for him, whenever he needed him, he would be there.

The client's phantom, who tried and failed to salve his extreme sleep disorder with alcohol, had hidden himself from the client. For eleven years the client had not known whether his phantom brother was alive. For eleven years the client, an alcoholic struggling to survive his own extreme sleep disorder, had made no effort to find him.

During the two hours of the client's five-session therapy the memory of his phantom had continuously intruded, a pressing memory and, with it, an urgent need to be believed about a past experience in an airport waiting room.

Dr. Darshan and his assistant could not keep the client focused upon procedure: to summon in a regulated loop of neurobiocontrol the "reward images" on the computer monitor before him: idyllic forest meadow, stream, trees, distant vague forms appearing according to scale of Adequate Total Reward achievement; blooming meadow flowers with hovering insect life, tree leaves, rippling stream surface and subsurface, stones in a streambed, a slender deer strangely hungry-looking, and pseudostars pulsing behind the hovering limbs of two omniscient hemlocks appearing according to scale of Ideal Total Reward. Deer Food, a chain-smoking green squirrel with a beer-gut, appeared according to outer-limit scales of Ideal Total Reward.

Electrodes (28—refer to cranial map) pasted to the client's scalp had previously recorded unprecedented abilities to regulate breath, blood pressure, heart rate, to eliminate inhibitory impulses of thought or feeling in order to concentrate attention upon the client's wished-for iterations of beauty intended to compensate for lifelong extreme sleep deprivation and absent deep sleep and REM stages of consciousness.

Session 9 goals were unrealized due to the client urgently emailing Deer Food during each therapeutic segment.
Noted by Dr. Darshan: *Unrevised client emails printed, filed. Phatic utterance characterized by voidance.*
Noted by Dr. Darshan: *The client Robert Lucens refers to himself as "Silence" and, at times, as "The Silence."*
Noted by Dr. Darshan: *For all future sessions, remove keyboard on computer monitor desk.*

8:18 AM
DF. DF, please stay, DF. There is something   a kind of not convincing story—I've never been able to make anyone believe it. I can't put it out of my head. I tell people and they sneer the way

they sneer at drinkers. Or they openly say *It doesn't add up, Mr. Silence.* I always think they are saying, It doesn't add hup.
It doesn't add hup.　　　It's the way I tell it. If I could tell it right if I could make you believe—but then maybe it just could never be true at all and believable. It seems not believable. I barely ever believe myself since I never slept more than eight hours a week my whole life like cold dashes and hyphens and spaces of Could are everywhere where the should-words for Should should be—
I hallucinated in the afternoons and late evenings saw blue pennants waving at me and on them　　　in them was whatever or whoever or wherever stood in front of me. I saw waving and sometimes whipping pennants light blue really pale　　　and in them on them might-things that might have been near me or in the far distance from me.　　　Hell　　　I think even in my crib I saw a crib-mobile of the pennants because my mother said I never slept right not even immediately after my birth. And my younger　　　brother　　　Saul　　　he never slept right. And the pediatrician who let me zip and unzip the smile of her special friend Zip-Me doll was of the opinion Saul was mentally retarded because he was still and because he was silent then not silent but screaming mostly like hawks make a scream that comes out of their entire bodies even the slenderest hollow pinfeathers. He was a sky-dweller. I was a ground-dweller. The pediatrician—the doll had no tongue no teeth except zipper-teeth—believed I was mentally retarded because I swayed swerved. When I crawled I kind of crawled through a tremulous something not there instead of toward something there. When I made my first words, Hup! Hup!, they flapped in vibrato ways they should not　　　and after I learned "Up!" I still said　　Hup.　　Today sometimes I'm over sixty now today sometimes I say Hup—　　　　　　I sound drunk　　　—when I mean "Up." I am trying I am making

79

a great effort but am not able to think of the difficult word Up
my thought will not go there. I say hupstairs, I say fill my cup
hup, I say   Anyway, I don't believe my own self too often. I
say, Onward and hupward! when I do not mean it. I am a kind of
liar is the truth but I have a blind friend Abraham who says every
person living in an altered reality alters reality. (He also says that
no matter what it is not acceptable to lie to yourself.)

8:49 AM
I have a blind friend Abraham—I could have mentioned
him should have I have just the one blind friend not lots of
them—there are never a lot of Abrahams that I see when I'm
seeing swarms and swarms. It is confusing to see just the one
Abraham who cannot see me. Abraham says lying—he is not a
liar himself—is not what Jesus would do who told his followers
Blessed is the Silence who will have words—who walked on words
when no one would believe he could—Jesus Iscariot Jesus Pilate
Jesus   Magdalene Jesus Mehitabel who asked for a hand to be
put inside the word in his side when it looked to others like it
was not   at all a word—a scratch is what people thought. I
told my friend Abraham this story I want you to hear. He would
not believe it. The whole thing doesn't take a lot of words and
probably is a proverb or a riddle and not a story at all—in the past
I didn't use enough of the right words.   The way I told it was my
whole problem. DF—DF—I'm going to put it down here because
I tried   to I know this now   I tried to tell it but I
needed to type it.

8:59 AM
I was at an airport terminal a smaller zone among the zones
a zonule   at night there the sounds were in a fog of

sound—like God flipping pages or burgers or surfing channels or dialing radio bands—noises and sounds noising sounds and leaching,   illuviating, accumulating. I had slept approx twelve hours in the past days 29 or so   so as usual I hallucinated the pennants thousands and tens of thousands of the pennants.   Near me or distant and coming nearer was a sleepwalking late-middle-age magpie muttering in his sleep and snoring—sleepstomping is what he was doing—to be accurate he was drumming his feet lightly.   I tried to read a bare place on the industrial green carpet worn down to illegible by flight-cancelled sleepers—but my brain invited more people-pennants blushing blue from the icy reflections of their cell-phone faces.

9:01 AM
He had a mostly black black-and-white checkered jacket on with a mostly white white-and-black checkered liner.

9:04 AM
I am getting this less wrong—because of you.   DF.   DF you might be what I needed I mean a listener a reader nonhuman approaching   and withdrawing   and withdrawing while you're reading me. The sleeping man a man older than me—he was definitely older probably by ten years but maybe more—he stomped, he skittered near but withdrew making a shrill gasp when he saw me—withdrew—withdrew into the soundfog—the shoveling-out sounds of flights about to land the shoveling-in sounds of flights outgoing   he withdrew   because of something about me—withdrew behind the voice of the pleather-zipper-woman across from me who was bluetoothing, *It is mine*— the rest of what she said was not clear though it was owner-like. Her sleeve- and ankle- and breast- and shoulder-zippers gnashed

and the zipper-pulls jangled. She wanted out of herself. A
toddler cicada two rows or so behind me kept telling someone he
wanted to see. The sleeping man was stomping again not at all
ominously—then ominously—then not at all—not at all.
The toddler giggled when I turned around and air-kissed him
and I stomped two beats before I was in rhythm with the sleeping
man stomping, the two of us stomping and then the toddler
stomping with passionate junglyness   stomping   toddler
thunder   the toddler was now a hundred-thousand
bannertoddlers stomping—the way an airport terminal never
sounds until until you hear it really stomping with the furling
unfurling pleather-zipper-woman and toddler and sleeping man
stomping—millions on the blue pennants and in the soundfog.

9:19 AM
I never can make anyone believe. The sleeping man stopped
stomping. He resembled me   I mean I resembled Saul and he
resembled Saul more than I—Saul and I looked unexactly alike
—he looked exactly like   that man   the shelver
there in Mini Bob's Mart. Saul had a job like the shelver once
and I knew about Saul and his full-time shit-paying job during
that time when Saul was living somewhere in car space   when
his home was in his car in an abandoned car lot. He hid himself
from me but was not good at hiding because I knew where he
worked and knew I could find him there. But I did not find him
there. I let him hide. I hid when it might be that Saul could find
me. I made people there promise not to tell that I asked about
Saul. He was a good worker wet-brain drunk and disoriented
on the job. He did not take days off sick—and was completely
dependable. He was not able to communicate right and was
liked—he was loved—loved is the word people used—I cannot

82

say that it has been used about me or ever will be—he was loved by customers by his boss by the big boss all of them   through an entire decade. He did not pray to any God but had a million benevolent Gods in mind was what he told people who worked with him who loved him who might have figured out that he lived in his car and then lived for a few days in dive apartments then in his car. Everyone in the zonule—throngs and throngs of people-pennants—wavered. It's not the right word   wavered how does anyone tell anything believable without the right word? They wavered as the man walked closer to me   and closer. The toddler wanted to see and so he walked at the man's side—he stood on the bare spot of carpet—quiet now the toddler looked at me closely and without any question in his throng of faces.

9:29 AM

It does not add up. Saul was dead. Saul has been dead for years. The sleeping man looked me up and down. He looked me over so that I would have to be in his gaze in the center of his gaze. The toddler   myriad toddlers   said   I want to see I want to see and stepped away from my side so he could see how the sleeping man saw. One Saul-crowd   one toddler-crowd crowd of pleather-zipper-woman crowd of arriving crowd of departing crowd in soundfog crowd of one waiting in God's zonule crowd of sleepwalking man asking me one question: *Brother? Is that you? Will you stay in sight?*

The client asked Deer Food, "How will I go home?"

"*Mercy*," said Deer Food, only faintly. "You want to go home?"

"No," the client said, "I mean yes. I should go home. I mean no.

No. But I want to know how."

"I've read your emails." Deer Food's volume was not significantly above Constant Zero.

"And?" the client asked.

"The story is not quite plausible," said Deer Food.

The client could barely hear his companion Deer Food as Deer Food asked, "What about that toddler? After it all. What did the toddler do?"

Mrs. Wiggins' altocumulus undulatus asperatus

Abraham   Dear Abraham I miss you   Abraham I see
Kudzu Serrucho and I miss you whenever I'm not the people in
my dreams I start to think you're the people in my dreams

Kudzu pulls off the saw's yellow and red cardboard sleeve—
sometimes you're the people in my dreams when I really am

the people in my dreams   your white cane stirring the floor

Kudzu says "Vamos por ella"—"Let's go for it" is what it means
and he leads me into the neighborhood a block east of Mr. P's
Hardware—Are you still blind Abraham?—you know what I
mean

Abraham you know what I mean   you could see how
Kudzu got the name   the trees in the neighborhood the bushes
and garden plants the dog-runs and doghouses the legs of real
slow dogs the garages and fences the satellite dishes   kudzu-
kudzu-kudzu he doesn't hold the saw at his side the kudzu is not
transition-averse like me   it hyphenates itself

on the Parkway bridges on the carwash hoses his chest is where
he holds it   Lifetime Warranty   his small fingers don't
fit the handle   fairly hard he spits on the blade   stares
takes a whiff of the steel—I can't help feeling it's a tiny world
this green grave this hardware store of hardware stories in which
a stranger utter stranger would have the same lung problems I
do—same bad-smelling sputum for which—I ask him "You take
pills?"—"Four" he says—for which *I* take pills   *four* pills every
day

"For what good?" he asks in a dreamSpanish loogie that has the
word *comezon* in it—laughs—I wouldn't know that word *comezon*
at all if I didn't get the exact same side effect   the itching
he wipes the saw blade off against his pants—his face is pissed
and beneficent   under the surface are white-hot green slender
vines

and slight stems of green lightning—I'm thinking of this woman
Mrs. Wiggins—this was on the Google News—the woman
who took a photo that made cloud physicists name a new cloud
category   Abraham remember when I used to read the
newspaper to you?   this Kindle thing will read it to you now
if there's no one to do that this Kindle thing has two Text-to-
Speech readers they call them T2Ss

I brought it up—new cloud category—two voices   male
and female   Tina Turner & The Boss   stalking the
neighborhood with Kudzu—making conversation—"Brand new
cloud category" I said—I added "I have two sons"   Kindle
doesn't tell you anything about the T2Ss I researched it   Tina
Bruce   He said "Look at them" and pointed to the row of black
plastic mailboxes on wood posts

many   many of them   "Sons too" he loogied   that was a fine
thing—his loogieSpanish—that we both had sons   two
he looked into the blade—held it in front of me so I could look

these modern mailboxes are a box and a long plastic sleeve that
fits over the post and is fixed to it with 12 woodscrews—to
cut one down you have to do some unscrewing or you have
to saw through the plastic   you haven't seen a loogie

86

have you? have you touched one?   when will we speak
of it Abraham? when I took the job as The Silence I had the
opportunity

to go mad and die

I took the opportunity   and then I lost the job and then they
hired The New Silence and I had the opportunity to move to
North Carolina

and go mad and die

and I took the opportunity   I can't promise that I'm ever
going to shut up about it

we had no screwdriver   a wind was picking up and he and I had
no screwdriver Abraham   you have an email address
Abraham but you're still blind as a tadpole Abraham
Abraham   the wind made me think of how a page of
newspaper turns by itself if you look at it hard and long on a
windy day after you've gone almost forever without sleeping
so someone   Abraham someone sighted or less blind than you
is reading this to you   hello Reader hello   Reader I was a
father and had two   two who loved me

& I was Abraham's reader   I was his T2S   We sawed right
through the plastic and Kudzu sawed down the sturdy mailboxes
of Mr. Martin and The Rorty Family   on the saw sleeve it said
the teeth were "induction hardened"   a hallucinatory blue
pennant flies where Kudzu's head should be they stay sharp longer
Abraham   Abraham it's true they stay sharper if they're

hardened by induction   and my theory—I told you—I've been
sleepless now for 56 years and you're the one who said that's like
112—my latest theory is that the pale blue pennant is what my
brain makes where it would have made a dream

Kudzu's head   is transparent liquid diamond blue   the
wind makes it whip and snap   the lapping tongues inside his
face thrash   four pills per day   expensive   I lay
down each mailbox's head and body   itching   itching but
not scratching they say   my sons say they can't ever think of me
the same way again

when he hacks up a few lung-flowers I hack up some too   a
vase of some kind would be nice

that would be nice about now because you want the last things to
last   it's not a tunnel   people will tell you that
the Reader—   not a real human—might have read that to you
I might have but Abraham   Abraham   at the end there
is a second-to-the-last thing   and there is a last thing

the second-to-the-last thing is a turning or a reaching   a
bending down   it's not white-lit not glorious not much   when
about 56 to 112 years of no-sleep have passed

you hear "Let's go for it—let's go for it—vamos por ella"
& the last thing is a simple sawing motion   8-point   20-
inch short cut   you lower the flag and close the mail mouth
it's not what you thought—not a tunnel or tube white-lit and
your whole life draining down   if you are   Abraham
Abraham   if you

are   being read to   who in hell is reading to you?

if I could like I used to   I'd read you a first article   and
then all the way through   all 296,111 related articles on
Mrs. Wiggins' one photo   altocumulus undulatus asperatus
she said it was like kudzu she said it was like no cloud she'd ever
seen.

A testicular self-examination

The Rio Grande should be repaired sooner or later because it's
a fuckin shame what happened to it which is not pretty. Irrigation
and all and no sturgeon any more and pubic hairs and pollution.
Harve Benedict, English 12, Elfego Baca High School

O hundreds and hundreds of Harves, your writing should have
been the death of me. It should have been.

In my memory I picture you and our off-white high-school trailer
classroom, the stinking heated air, imbalanced orange plastic chairs and
desks, manic, twitching, ricocheting fluorescence, spittled spatter-pattern
tiles, and smeared chalkboards. More alone with my lesson plans than I
had planned, I pay tribute, seat you, take attendance, mark you present
but gone.

Gone. And missed.

Even the ass-kissing or dispassionate or self-obsessed wasted-
slacker slumming hopeless worst of you Harves are still dangerously
present in me.

For the record, I should mark down that my grade books were
amiss because I made a place across twelve columns to record my sales,
your costs, and, at my whim, the other matters at hand.

I had slots in my books for the good shit, for the shit, for the
rewrite second shot, for the wasted second shot. I had a slot I could make
you fit.

I have all the grade books. In thirty years of teaching they are the
only books I wrote.

You knew firsthand my forms of insult to The Teaching
Profession, so you would understand that I remember you best just when
I have my pants around my ankles, my testicles in hand, fumbling with
my most ordinary means of communication, my praxis and true praxis,

90

my imagined spheres of influence, my twin inadequate vocabularies, my theses, my parallel narratives and my pure lyric impulses, my flesh's synonyms and soul's antonyms. My syllabi.

My syllabi. There, that clarifies, that has a ring.

I willed the essays you wrote to define but not defy the audience. I wanted your words, I willed them to have the true ring; you wished them to ring true. And because I had been taught the dry, exhausted world would operate neither on beauty's truth nor truth's beauty, I knew from the beginning what curriculum I would teach you.

So, I repeat, I repeat myself as I self-examine, passing my fingertips like blind mandibles over the puckered seam of my scrotum to discover the drama growing upon the drama within. Oh, I imagine I see you, see your eyes spin, the light in them dimming, as they always did when, in my less naked days, I exercised my prerogatives and lectured at you, poking parts of the enlarged diagrammed sentence I pinned to the cork strip at the top of the scored chalkboard.

Are you as embarrassed as I am by this admission into evidence of my two mortgages, two secret business files, yang and yang, And and Ampersand, my letter home and letter back, my Brothers Grimm, my grim brothers? Embarrassing.

It is embarrassing. Goddamn.

It is—and it was then. O hundreds and hundreds of Harves, I bent your attention from the words you had written to what I called "the matter at hand" to which we gave our concentration whether or not your essay was a yelp in the dark, a wild song meant to break you from the ranks of the marching.

I dynamited the secret daily deepening love for learning inside any of you who had the elemental need for beauty and brutality within. Strictly according to my orders, you obediently rode your hands and the nubs of your pens over the surface of the page in order to not enter, not swim in where your unsleeping secrets and first and final doubts might appear unhidden.

Your sparking faces reignite in my memory, and will not be drowned out as I drowned them out then. Self-loathing, self-loving, self-avoiding, I am self-examining, self-examining my classifieds, my want ads, questioning, and indulging, indulging and indulging my excesses of self-intimacy.

My motives will never be unugly, will they? No one knows as you do that what compassion I lacked made me ask you back any question you asked.

In a race against you dambreakers, I made dams. Wanting language to have use, I demanded you learn how to change its natural course, to divert it, drain every untamed cubic foot. Of course. You knew, know, that.

Do you remember? When you picture me, is this what you picture?

Showered and powdered. A midday desert storm makes the bathroom light fixture tremble, and the water swirling down the drain flashes at me like a whip snake.

The lights in my home are lowered and curtains drawn. I know my curriculum, my medical routine as one of the "predisposed," as one of cancer's pupils.

Goddamn. Oh, I do not want to remember, but I remember the hundreds of sentence-suffering student conferences with my dented, unbalanced metal desk between us in my designated space of the giant communal faculty office.

There was weed and fast-food smell on you, Harve. Eyes and cheeks blood-webbed, the backs of your neck and hands sunburned and your palms blistered.

Nothing on either side of "because" seemed to flow right for you. O Harve, Harve Discussion-Killer, Harve Chain-Yanker—son of fourth-generation Mesilla Valley cotton farmers—class of '90? '91?—second-sem junior Goth metalhead brilliant nonachiever—emerald goatee, emerald short spiked hair, mucus-coated skull ring hanging from your septum.

You wrote, *The Rio Grande should be fixed because it's a fuckin shame what happened to it.*

"Harve," I said, "what part should be repaired? It's a big river."

You said, "The whole thing." I said, "It's a long river."

You said, "Repair it, then. Don't fix it."

"It's best to focus, Harve." "Fuck you," you said.

"And when—you should say when." I asked, "Well, Harve?"

"Yeah? Yeah, yeah."

"Listen. Can you put 'when' in?"

You said, "Fuck you." I said, "Would you put 'when' in?"

You pinched the feet of the crucified Christ on your homemade earring, and you kind of put "when" in: *The Rio Grande should be repaired sooner or later because it's a fuckin shame what happened to it which is not pretty.*

"That's better," I said, not believing my own words. Believing only in complete sentences, I disliked your added fragment, which you would not change: *Irrigation and all and no sturgeon any more and pubic hairs and pollution.*

O Harve, O hundreds and hundreds—with any luck, you haven't thought of me for years. I wish this for you: that I am dismissed, expelled, that I never come to mind, that I am your lost but replaceable crutch tips, your unrefillable prescriptions, the lecture notes you would not take, the higher grade you would not get.

O you hundreds and hundreds of Harves missing the "because" gene. I have poured you in and poured you out of my bifocal lenses, I have insisted that we bow to the matter at hand, the curriculum, the curriculum, but I have needed, wanted your flooding truth to kill what I have been. For thirty years.

Now, I have my immutable troubles and truths, such as they are,

93

unwarranted radials, good-as-new-unrebuilt-used hard disk drives, my riches, my riches, out in the poor light, though I understand that looking will not help me. I go by touch.

For thirty years I have made the same mean wrong wishes—to identify instead of know—to know instead of feel and know—to reach instead of search—and a fourth goal I could not or would not name: to put an end to anything that simply is. You, my matter at hand, my own unproductive, overeager metastasizing cells, have tumesced in me for three decades of daily sweet assault upon my most sacrosanct first principles of utility.

You have taught me. You have taught me.

How blessedly terrifying to search for and reach you, the truths gathering, gathering within me. You have grown upon and will destroy me.

Notes on his poems by a guy who observed them in their natural habitat.

His poems were skunky. His skunky poems gorged
upon flowers at the edge of ponds swarming with frog
eggs in their cloudy sheaths. His poems slept where
they ate. Often, they slept upon the stubble of what
they had eaten. Whatever sang nearby they sang, too,
without imitating. They drooled. Bristled. Scratched
themselves in moonstruck pleasure. Hissed. Hucked
up tar. Hucked up lint. Hucked it down. They could
not keep their tongues in their mouths or out of their
own clover-scented anuses. They were warren-born
with their sticky eyes and ears open. They shed in all
seasons. For their young they wove warming blankets
from their belly hair. If they were frightened while they
were gorging upon the roots of succulent water plants
they ran the way furred things run. They found hiding
places where they could shit and re-ingest in peace.
They hid with their obsidian eyes closed. They gave
themselves permission to tunnel in. Dreamed where
they grazed. Grazed where they dreamed. They pushed
their twitching noses into the marshy places. At the
tops of their heads were predator-avoidance mating-
behavior black hair-splotches, mysterious growths that
they could thrust back, thrust forward. If you ever saw
their alert splotches, you miss them. Now and then,
you miss the poems. Their unhandsome hind legs made
bounding possible. They bounded. They bounded
while they slept. They were low on the food chain,
these poems, the favored snack of predacious poems.
They were of an order called Orlenorpha, not thought
important to remember until its extinction.

The last things we said

The last things we said to each other after hours of calling out, knocking walls, wild thumping around, pointless strategizing, no cell phone reception, laughing, loud chilled laughing, urinating so satisfying we called it The Rapture—lots of urinating against the sealed door, and then The Need to, but drained, nothing, none, and both of us each of us screaming at the sealed door—perfect seal, weak screaming, a session of cell-phone picture-taking, erasing two, keeping three, some loving things said and real beautiful, some things that were not, some weeping, some retracting of the smart hate, shivering, apologizing for the stupid love (this was before the lavaging) (this was before the amputating, way before), no cell reception, *no cell reception*, angry about it, cell phone camera working fine, furiously thankful for that, one of us hallucinating black-licorice-flavored blood pumping in the circulatory system of the word *bell*, one of us flicking his eyelids with his thumbs to make them ping, and taking some cell-phone head-shots, a dozen at least, the other asking What are we doing? and the other What are we doing next? asking whether or not that was more rain hitting the roof so hard, and asking, like it was the first time, Was that more rain? forgetting, asking, stripping himself naked at the end, hard to talk, mouth not exactly working, and asking himself and me, And?—and you'd think we'd talk about our loved ones, say their names, we did, we said the words which made everything good but not right—a word you don't have locks you down until you have it, kills you as soon as you do, and each of us both of us went burrowing into soft, warm imaginary forest soil, grubbing down, it's how freezing goes, you become a grub, a C shape, you grub down, you burrow down doing the grub-worm disco in the refrigeration unit of the Schwan's truck, the feeble, silver-dreadlocked, buggy, bitch trucker's rig which was half-on half-off the shoulder of I-40 at Old Fort, we couldn't believe it, you know (we had a load to deliver, you know?), couldn't believe we stopped for the trucker, but there she was—clear as day—couldn't believe we walked right to her (stitched on her white jumper the name "*Al*"), said to us, "Pre-mix"—her whole desperate speech in total—smoothed the black long-sleeves of her t-shirt, shuffled herself off balance, like a buggy stuffed bird, asked us to unseal her doors, looked down at her nurse-type black shoes, at her cracked pink driving gloves, sent us in, what were we thinking pulling over our seventeen tons of crushed three-quarter in a bad rainstorm, craned her neck in the direction of her trouble—sent us in—we felt like an offering, we had a bad feeling under the good feeling we both and each felt when the light came on, the motion-sensitive kind, the small amber light—we could see the hives of shelving, the waffled floor and ceiling, the mounted poster of a stoned Black Jesus so natural we both thought, *Fantastic!* which was when she sealed the doors behind us, happened fast, a certain compartment inside—outside another compartment—possibly she used a remote control—probably—before the poor thing stepped into the road, got punched out of the world with us trembling inside her unit, saying some things, a few more fairly unsurprising things, checking the cell, checking and checking it, and saying things before we could barely talk at all, had something left, had nothing, and, then, died saying the last things:

> He asked, "Dry barbecue? Or wet?"
> "Well. Wet, I guess."
> "Wet it is. You got to grow up with dry to have an appreciation. *Check* it."

> "What was it with those nurse's shoes?"

> "Shiny."
> "And dreads? Kinda silver-white. Silvery white. And those gloves. Jesus-Mary-"

> "-Joseph."

97

"Couldn't believe it, you know."

"Me neither. Check it. Please. *Please*."

"There's no reception, man. Nothin."

"Pork? Or beef?"

"Come on."

"Pork, huh?"

"Well."

"Are rasta-trucker-nurses supposed to kill guys like us? That breaks a couple vows at least."

"She was buggy, that's all. She didn't mean to kill us. She forgot us soon as we were inside."

"Forever."

"Forgot us forever."

"She didn't forget The Product—not her damn Pre-mix."

"Check it. Check it."

"Come on."

"Check it. What *is* Pre-mix?"

"It's what you—nothing, there's nothing—that's it. My hands—my fingers are falling off—I'm not checking it again—pre-mix is what you put in before. Before it's fish paste, before it's shrimp sauce."

"So."

"So."

"All the satellites. I'm hot. Christ. Christ. My skin burns. The cables and towers and dishes, nationwide networks, package deals, all the bundling. I'm going to have to kill me some Verizon people if I—"

"That was it, right? The word 'bundle.'"

"Right."

"The whole reason to go with Verizon."

"'Bundle.'"

"It's like that."

"It's hot. Burns. Burns. Christ. Christ, it burns like fire on a popsicle."

"I got—who *is* that? Is that Bob Marley?—I got something left."

"I got nothin."

"That's—he's—good luck!"

"I got nothin."

"Take one. Take a picture of him."

"Well. My hands."

"Oh."

"A shame."

"It would've looked just like him."

"I'm goin in."

"Down?"

"Down."

"Hard to get in."

"You down yet?"
"Almost."

"Better?"
"Better."
"Better?"
"Better."

"Better?"
"Good."
"Whew!"
"Whew."

"How far down?"

"I'm down," he said. "I'm all in. You?"
"I'm in."

**

And this is what we said, this is every last word

we said while the two young EMTs re-warmed us in the kitchen of the
Burger Time—they were improvising because the nearest emergency
room was too far off and the storm not letting up, and they could tell
we were almost finished, because it turns out you can die pretty fast
right after you die by freezing inside a refrigeration truck, so they were
trying to bring us to room temp, one whispering "Core," and the other
"Cube," and someone from the bottom of a clicking, roaring falls said,
"Shh. Shhhh"—they were trying to go slow, and they were, they were

uncurling us the best they could, they were slow-flexing the tips of our grub fingers and the tips of our grub toes, and they opened our pinging eyelids, looked in, slid them closed—sweet-pure pinging sounds—we were straightened slow and slow-stretched, flattened, saturated in the warm fry grease rubbed over our segments, we were remembering The Rapture while there was discussion between them and the manager about the dishwasher, whether it could be retooled fast enough—then fingers were held at the eight- and two-o'clock position on our groins—— and one said, "Lavage"—and the next thing the other did was cut into our guts so they could pull it all out or warm-rinse the whole internal works, and one calmly said, "Port," and the other, in the same calm voice, "Exit," and at the rim of a gorge someone said, "Meedyum—nopeyeah—meedyum," but "lavage" was in us—lavage—lavage—what a word, with lava in it—and that's—that's, that's—it made you want to taste a picture of yourself, and it made you love the name Al, and until the word was done to us, until we were each other's canyon and coffin, we never would have thought about the ah in it, the humidity of that—would we have thought about that?—come on—come *on*—how?—we wouldn't've, couldn't've— come on—it's against the odds, a word going inside us that way when we were each and both re-cooled in the walk-in, and re-warmed near but not under the food-warming lamps which were *amber*—amber—no kidding—after death you stop exaggerating—and I wondered where was the cell, the shots we took, where was the dead trucker and what was The Product in her unit, and they repeated the process—lamps, walk-in, lamps—trying to save us—like you can't do sometimes, like sometimes you can't do—and I learned later that the cell was never found—The Product was pre-mix for ice cream—the old thing flew out of her bright shoes and higher than the pines, and home—and after hours of lavage— what a word, man, there aren't a million words as good—after I was a functioning human fountain and believed I could live, after I asked, "And my friend?" that was when I smelled the mustard of the world, and not the mild kind, it was on the young man's upper lip, his hands, my brain, the plastic-pack perfect mustard of the world, and his voice was burger-muffled when the young man said, "Now, look," and repeated it, so I looked, I said, "*But. I remember*—" then the young man said, "There's just you—" then I said, "—*every word*."

He said, "AT&T next time."

I said, "Or T-Mobile."
"How about—"
"—that new one—Vonage?"
"Oh! Oh. Yeah. *Vonage*."

He said, "There was something funny about her."
I said, "Always is."

"The driving gloves?"
"Well."
"Were they really pink?"
"Yeah."
"Shoes?"
"Shiny black."

"We sure went down, didn't we?"
"Way down. You good?"
"I'm good."
"It's good down there."

"It is. It's good."

"Well."
"Couldn't believe it, you know."
"Me neither."

I said, "You see her, too?"
He said, "Clear as day."

Oh, how glad and happy when we meet

December 31, 2011

Happy holiday, Mrs. Minerva-Jones Slattern Lundsford,

      Remain calm. This IS a holdup. It does not involve large amounts. It would not come natural to me to be a violent person—I am a customer here at Wells Fargo. I was a customer here: Mr. Tim Ed Lamb, account closed in March 2008. Look that up. Go ahead, search that on your computer. Calmly now. No kidding—I want you to search for "Mr. Lamb" in order to buy time to read this note and come to know me, and to follow my written directions. Search completed? I am kind of messing with you. It is not a funny joke, is it? Do not be sore at me. This is the fourth winter here that everybody says is the worst ever winter in Buncombe County. Until we are unfrozen, we are frozen goods, and we do not know for how long. Life comes down to a question, Minerva-Jones. I will come to that—the question. After we have successfully robbed this stagecoach, feel free to share this letter with others. I will not mind if you do. I have not rounded off the exact amount of this withdrawal of seventy dollars and seventy cents. The way the numbers work out feels good. Like a good sign. The car battery, AutoCraft Perma-Power, the top of the line, 3 yr. warranty, costs $212.10, total. Life comes down to a question. Seventy dollars and seventy cents at your station. The same amount at Mrs. Maud Ardent's station. Same at Emily Sparks' station. Two-one-two-one-zero and seven-zero-seven-zero times three. Good numbers. A good sign. It figures out, it adds up, it comes down to a question you have to answer: *What if it broke?* You can see I understand you, I have come here to Wells Fargo twice a week like I still had business here, and I have looked at you, written some notes down. You laugh a lot. But no pretending or fake politeness. Something a little pleasant sets you off. Off-color sets you off but not as good as full-color. Something inside sets you off. Nobody has said anything and nothing has happened—and you get a cockeyed smile. And it opens up. It has been good to come in here so I could see that. Thank you, Minerva-Jones. What if I could not see that?

Life would not be the same. *What if what you had to have broke? What if it broke?* You have got to answer or the winter comes and you are done for. There is not an app. There is no app for holdups. We are on our own, and one font size is as good as another in this situation. This font is pretty large. I hope it is large enough. I do always look like this, like a thawed face was glued onto a frozen face. If there is a mug shot or a line-up, I will look like this, like I look in that little flipswitch on the car mirror: day is back there and, sixty-two years later: night. You're wondering about my sunglasses. I wear them because of light sensitivity. My dad, Reverend Butch Alpert, gave me them. They are something that is left when no charge is left. I suppose I am a threat. I do not feel like it. I feel a common thread. I do not know, I have no way to know if right at this part you are not sore at me and you are smiling. Or if you are sore at me and not smiling. Or sore at me and smiling. This is a good day for you and me and Mrs. Ardent and Miss Sparks. You have your stations. I have my lot. Together, we are robbing a bank and the reason why is so that a '99 Ford Taurus will rise again. It is not such a bad world. It is not so bad. I will take the cash envelope now. Please.

Very sincerely, and signed with my real name,
Herb Alpert

Merry Late Xmas, Mrs. Maud Ardent,

    It is better not to look up at me. Look over—your right, my left—at Mrs. Minerva-Jones Slattern Lundsford. She is in on this. It is not so terrible to be an accomplice. Look again. My guess is that she has laughed and that it is not a nervous laugh or panicky or anything. Call her up on your email so that you look like you are computing while you are reading this holdup note. Stop right here. Stop reading. Okay. Read. I want you to send her an email, a six-word email. Write "Cloggers do it heel and toe." And there it is. (I would bet my battery it is there: Minerva-Jones' smile.) You are lucky to work here. You have sent the email? Return to your robbery instructions. At your left, my right is Emily Sparks who also clogs. One branch bank with two cloggers on the same shift is a pleasant surprise. It is a sign. She will give me seventy dollars and seventy cents, exactly the same as you. Stop right here. Stop reading. That rubber-coated motorized device at the end of my arm was my hand. It is my hand. It is good for typing, better for typing than my right hand which was not bad enough to be replaced but which I cannot trust. Nerve damage. I have lost all trust in it even though I was right-handed once. By this time, Minerva-Jones has returned your email. Read it. Do not read it to me. Remain friendly toward me. Do not flirt. I can tell you what she has written. She has written, "It is not a large amount." She has written, "Maud, when I saw you and Emily clogging at Fiddlin' Pig, I thought, Fantastic! The basic and the drag-slide, the men in their black buck-taps, the whole vine slurring, the whole figure weaving, the kicks, the slapbacks, the swivels and triple stomps, and Emily's spine straight as a post and you have—how old are you, Maud?—you have the skinniest white legs. Well, I guess. Dancing like that. And your satin black pettipants showing and your fluffing red petticoats. Fantastic!" That Minerva-Jones. There is something inside. Whatever is inside resembles me. As a result, I know what she has written. It sounds like me. What is there about our lives, Mrs. Maud Ardent, that is not fantastic? All of it is. And you. You are probably late sixties, but you are a bank-teller-clogger-robber. That is a lot of metal on the toes and heels of your white lace-up oxfords. That is a lot of fantastic lipstick and fantastic nail polish, and no one but Emily Sparks—and, now, Minerva-Jones—compliments you on it. It is time to respond to Minerva-Jones' return email. It is time to flirt with me. It is time to tap. Here is the list. 1) Last things first: do some flat footing there under the counter—so I can hear it. 2) Show me your nails. I promise I will not take your hand in my rubber clamp. Hold your nails out for me so we can look at them together longer than we should. Mine was a hand once. 3) Type these exact words in email to Minerva-Jones: *That was me tapping. He made me tap. He is attracted to me in an animal way.* We have been together so long, Maud. We have been together longer than the normal transaction. It might cause suspicion. Do you think it will? Stick-ups go wrong when they go too fast, when they lack intimacy. This is my first, but I think that my theory is probably true. A few years back, you wrote your full name, notarized, on my loan, which was my amputation loan. Two amputation procedures. Left hand. Right foot. The *Citizen-Times* told it wrong. There were two of us who froze to death inside the Schwan's delivery truck. My co-driver died. He could not go that deep in, that far down, and come back. They left him out. They left out that while I was in ICU I was fired. If I do not succeed in our affair. If they ask whether I acted alone. If they cannot believe I did. If you have been seen flirting with me, and you <u>have</u> been seen at least by Minerva-Jones—flirting with me. If there are letters you wrote to me that are perfectly forged pure poems of lust with your forged signature on them, a flawless forgery made by a rubber clamp so precise it can tweeze a mouse's eyebrows. If I am sentenced to a warm cell in a state prison where I do not depend on one car battery in one car that has been my home since I closed my account here, since I have had one question which my life depends on. Stop reading. Stop. Send this email to Emily Sparks: *A man is coming to your station. He has seen us clog and he is robbing this bank and I am helping him and it does not involve a large amount. It does not involve my love for him. It does not involve Minerva-Jones. But—see? See how happy it makes her? He has a motorized clamp. He will give you instructions.* Send it. Now, look at me. You can see that my death really changed my life. I died and was completely revived. It was the most life-changing thing in my whole life. This letter implicates you. I do not want that. Put this letter in the envelope with the $70.70. Is Minerva-Jones looking at you? Is she laughing like a broken fiddle? What are we doing? What are we doing next? You and I. We were so good together.

With no regrets,
Red-Head Sammy

Dear Miss Emily Sparks,

      Hello. I am glad to make your acquaintance. As you know, together we are withdrawing a small amount of money. I have come to your station with the core of me rumbling, knocking, and numbering, Emily. After all this time, I am here. You have been in a certain station of my dreams. Have you noticed that? Think of it. I have a car that wants to run. There is a wooden floor at the Fiddlin' Pig. If I ask you for $70.70 that sounds right. You have heard it before; the sound of the car, the sound of the floor under the basic shuffle and tap, the numbers seven-o seven-o. The gas-whoosh stovetop sound of Minerva-Jones' laughter, which comes from inside her where I am fairly sure I have been curled up and dreaming since the first time she swallowed her own spit. I have thought of that, of her, of Mrs. Maud Ardent, of you, have stood here in this bank at this branch a little while almost every day. It is pleasant here. My account was closed two years ago. Wells Fargo has a good men's restroom, a stagecoach theme, amber lighting. I have done no business here, so you have not noticed me though you have noticed that I am there. I have a clamp, a spring in my step that is a real spring with a robotic tendon. Your mind wanders out beyond your station but never as long as a transaction that you could call real. Do you hear Maud tapping? That actually is her tapping "Arkansas Traveler." I am guessing that. But I am pretty sure. It is a pleasant thing. A sign. She has not told you I am a fan of the Soco Gap Cloggers, but I am. In the East Asheville Library it is warm, but it is patrolled by Officers Nichols and Haywell. I have typed and printed letters there. I have conducted clog research there. I have put myself there. I have been removed. As for the Fiddlin' Pig—on nights when I have not had even enough to buy one side order of deep-fried pickles, I have paid my cover fee. There are things you can sell. You let them go. It is no different than losing a hand or a foot or a friend, a guy who was a real friend. No different than if they tell you you had no friend to lose, there was no co-driver, there never was, that you worked for Schwan and not for Stone Supply. If they tell you your mind is not what it was, and they "let you go," but it was one of your four part-time jobs, so you can move on, you can tell Schwan thank you for the twenty-seven part-time years of frozen goods, thank you, you brought out the best in me and my co-driver. You can tell Schwan thank you, I mean that, thank you, the customers who like the flounder were my least favorites, that is what I can tell you, thank you, thank you, the ice cream customers were the best. If the ex, who had a thing about wearing pink leather gloves, and her new wealthy husband in a mansion like the monster mansion for which your retirement income pays the mortgage. If the ex and the ex's man Al thought an amputation loan to you was a bad idea. If the ex said, You've lost the other three jobs, haven't you? If the ex telephoned you back to say you should go to a bank, it is ridiculously easy to get a bank loan these days. If you explained that you would have jingle-taps on your new foot and a precision clamp hand and would be employable again, but only the words "mid-life crisis" and "economic collapse" came from the other end of the line. I am glad to do this, to jump from my horse onto the Wells Fargo stagecoach, to watch you jump. And Minerva-Jones. And Maud who has landed not so good, and is kind of chuckling. I am glad to do this with women since. I have never done this since. It is different since. I have not been held and I have not held a woman since. It is hard to let go. After you give me the $70.70. Give it to me in a calm and businesslike and romantic way. After this transaction. Tell me what you want. After you have told me. Look at me. It is all right. Tell me what you want. Are you sure that is what you want? No one can ever give you that. I will now leave through the front door. I will not return to this branch. Keep looking at me. Far down, deep in. Like you're holding me.

In love,
Bascom Lamar Morris

Title from "I'll Fly Away," Albert E. Brumley

"On the wire, Boys."

Bill told the band he was holding us back from the Grand Ole Opry. The Opry hadn't got through its hick and hillbilly ways enough to be ready for the Foggy Mountain Boys. He put it something like that. At a later time, he held us back from recording for the Beverly Hillbillies TV show. Same problem. We had our doubts, of course, since we were dividing up sixty bucks a night and could've learned to like six hundred. My wife said we were done if I wasn't done with him and the band and the never-ending touring for next to nothing. The nicest thing I ever got her was the suitcase that I bought her. And then she moved to Tennessee, a place I hope to never see again. When it was time to record for the TV show and knock the Opry on its rear, we did it because Bill said it, simple as that, and, he reminded us, he was the leader of the outfit no matter what.

After a little bit, our money didn't double or triple. What's the word you use for hauling trainloads more dough than you have pockets for? It isn't bragging since it's true: we made the first million-sale album in bluegrass history. Shouldn't something have changed? And did it some? *On the wire, Boys*, he'd say and at the right moment in the song we all lowered and tucked in our instruments, landed without a flutter, leaned in. *That's how*, he'd say, which was our cue to fall back. Bill, always the leader, made the rules. Plenty of old rules to remember, new ones to learn. Here's one. We weren't—no matter what—allowed to tune our instruments on the stage. *Tune them when you're off the boards*, he said, *and I mean perfect as perfect can be*. He wasn't kidding either—you can ask around. The idea was that we would start out in tune, each one. And fall out together.

A 4 oz. can of story

I'm guessing now, but I bet being an inflatable can of Sprite is hard out there in the heat, the rain. The heat inside. I thought about the heat inside that outfit.

I saw you dancing your contents, shaking yourself, and spinning like no soda should ever do. I saw you pulling at your tab, leaning down to pour in front of Oteengles supermarket. I saw your weird chalk wet spots on the pavement. You were a pissed off Sprite. That was the effect. I saw you disco-lift your arms and do kung-fu kicks in your sparkling nylons.

It all scares the babies. Can you see that through your little fabric screen? It scares the little shitters for life.

I know you're short, not so bright, but I don't like the idea of you being a soft drink, brother. I don't like the danger of you falling and—it's steep there, you notice that?—and what if you went rolling down the lot right into traffic. Think of it.

But if you're going to be a soda out in the rain and the heat have you thought that maybe you ought to be a smoother drink, cooler, more effervescent?

Exchange the white gloves for black. That would be good.

Wipe the birdcrap from your rim. Be less bouncy in the legs. Keep your arms down, your hands off your tab.

Think of the babies.

There is a long-time-ago-happy-big-sister-little-brother story I tell myself. About you and me. And duct tape. I almost believe it sometimes. I like that I made it up. I like that I sealed it in. I like that you can be pried open with your own hands. You're not a giant rubber, not a soda, not really, but pretty lifelike when you're angry.

I like seeing you make a new start. I like that. What business of mine is the soda business?

Hey now. Hey. I don't have to like what you are in your can of story.

Me? I'd rather be soup myself. Think of it. If I could be stirred like a planet, if I could boil over on the range. If I could be kissed and then sipped from a spoon by a man with a rocket in his pocket (if you know what I mean). Someone like Probably Jesus without him being so religious.

It would be good to be soup. After the story silt was scraped out, when I was completely empty, I would like to admit, *That's all there is to me.*

In case they bring us some, here is a spoon. Not a good one. In case it is enough for a bowl and not a cup, here is a cup. Small. Isn't it small though?

In case we spill, here is a paper napkin.

An 8 oz. can of story

Too much can for this six ounces of chicken &—think of it: they put so few in. You look. It's like a condemned planetarium or an empty night sky.

Look all you want, you won't find them—seems like I'm making a joke or a prayer in a can of joke on a pew that stinks because that's what Probably Jesus would do.

I don't know.

Am I joking?

It shouldn't matter because it costs less than nothing—marked Expired, marked Do Not Sell after the Second Coming. Too much *can* for this much can—think of it: they put in almost no chickenfleshy gummy somethings—but they feel fine about calling it Chicken Ampersand.

Why will people who *have* leave out so much for people who would love to have one full serving?

I don't think—much—about them. I'm trying not to think.

Think of it: do I ever think about them? I don't know. I don't know. What am I thinking poking into this much can? That does not sound like what I mean.

What I mean is you feel the price you paid is worth it if you paid nothing. And I mean that. I have parted my hair and found more fine dining living in my scalp than this. Outside the bakery I had loaves of air that were better. Outside the brewery, brewy gulps of hoppy gas coming from people's asses.

You look. You think what might've gone in. Am I thinking? I'm trying not to think.

I don't know.

What might have gone in?

Think of it: life is hard enough if it was "Chicken."

Think of it: "Chicken &."

Chicken &.

Chicken &.

And, hungry as I am, I don't want it to be only Chicken.

Bless us, O Lord, for these 6 of the advertised 8 ounces.

Bless us, but would you—would you think of it. What if it all was here. Imagine: Chicken &.

Stars.

The Y

Most of us in the Y Senior Rehab began self-medicating—okay, call it what it is—we started drinking—in our seventies. The wrong prescriptions for acceptance got to be too much for us to accept. And now, since you're joining, and since I'm the one who's been told to give you the big picture, picture this: a bunch of us brain-compromised, diabetic, brother-less, sister-less, wife- and husband-less, Viagra-less and nut-less and breast-less, arthritic and asthmatic, palsied, hemorrhoidal, balding, cancer-carved, triple-bypassed drunks stagger in every Monday morning at five on our own wrecked wills to learn how to get our cold feet into the shallow end again. Sound fun?

Our mothers are not alive and here to drive us at dawn to the unlit gravel apron around the corrugated steel Quonset hut. No one holds and then lets go of our clean hands, and nods us sternly towards the iron gate and the iron door. At the entrance to the shadowy locker room the Y matron astride a high gray metal stool hands out towels, thin towels, blue chits and blue pool baskets. Like children, we men talk about her and lose our place talking about her as we strip and shower with phlegmy bars of off-brand soap from our own wet pink plastic snap-close boxes, and believe, every morning, believe the cold water might turn hot if we turn the handle to H and hold it.

"She looks at us funny," we say. "She's gotta be over ninety." "D'you think that's her '70 Mustang out there?"

We shrink under the shower's stinging slivers of ice and whimper a little as we put on our draw-string mesh-lined swimming boxers.

Someone asks, "You serve?" Someone answers, "Patton's army." And the guy who always says it, says, "We need some heat in here."

We say stuff like that. What you'd expect. But there's rungs of silence when we can't track, different rungs of lag for different men, and rungs where the regret goes because some of us have enough memory left to feel regret. Our buoys of collapsing waistline fat and our hairy, fallen balls and fallen butt cheeks were unfallen once and our prostates soft as sugar packets, and our shrunken pricks had fresher, innocent faces and necks. We step into the chilly concrete inch-deep squares of disinfectant footbath. We walk out of the bunker. We don't just go past the Pool Rules. We read.

And we breathe quiet as birthday candles, and recite the rules to ourselves as if for the first time.

In the echoing, noxious room the girls our age are already in line at the edge of the pool. Their suits and ours: red. Red is the rule. They gaze into the water, their pale mouths closed, slack jaws clenched, faces faking bravery, and their still, sleeping open hands swing at their sides. Their toes and goosebumped feet flatten, their feet, their painted toes, the old mandogs know it is hard to love those toes, wrinkled feet flattened against the blue speckled tiles. In their red one-pieces, which fit their waists but not their chests, or their chests but not their waists, they are as childlike as they were at six. Sound fun yet? Maybe it is. We have no hungering awe of their necks and nipples and breasts and hips or the cloth-hidden silent mouths of their sex, or, for that matter, their mouths at all. We feel too something, too—something—too innocent for that. Chalk it up to the cold, the hour, the moon's southing, the Y's faded red ceiling paint flaking, steadily snowing banjo-plunking pink flakes that smell like Arbuckle coffee, taste like the holler. And they nod at us, they straighten up, they wave. Afterwards, at home and alone, you think, Ancient. Beautiful. But there at the Y no one flirts or jokes or lets on, anyway, that there is any romance in it. No one says anything that might dispel the reverberating wasp-murmuring of the caged overhead lamps and the water lapping the pool lip and making licking sounds along the windowless rubbery white walls of cinderblock. No talk. No glasses in our hands. No golf clubs. No bottles pouring. Some of us adjust our suits, but that can make your skin a bad fit, so we readjust. When the Y matron, our coach, enters, she has showered. Her burr-cut hair is dripping wet. If your hair is dry, she glares, she sends you back. If your suit is immodest or too poor a fit, she'll tell you.

She'll tell you, "Shave that" and—woman or man—point to your hairy chest, back, face, thighs, crotch where the offense against smoothness could make you ineligible for her class. "Straighten up," she says if you're more bent than you have right to be. Her erupting varicose veins have spread over every wall and awning of the crumbling ruin of her body. Magnificent blue mansion, older than the oldest of us. She told us once and only once, "You are all pathetic puppies. When I was your age I was pathetic, too—don't sweat it." As if she were the mother of our mothers, she lines us up on either pool side, showing us how our feet go and where our feet go, and—picture this: we put our feet that way, every one of us. We obey. We already know we should be an arm's-length apart. So.

Wobbling a little, we stretch our arms out to measure the distance, which is just enough closeness, all the closeness we desire, and all she will permit. She tells us to bend at the waist and crouch at the knees. "I said bend, Mister. Don't take a bow."

When she commands, "Dry crawl," we rotate our arms and move our heads from this side to that and breathe in and blow out. When she says to stop you'd better. "Who told you it was fair or that it was fun?" Now that you've paid your fee to join, you'll see what you've done. If you're out of turn, she turns your head for you in her cold, clean motherly hands. She clasps your waist and grabs up and straightens your wrists, unfanning your fingers, pushing down your lower back, demanding that you move slower, reach further, roll your shoulders into the stroke and stroke smoothly and lift and lower your hips. Not a single instinct in us makes this anything more than what it is—swimming out of water, imagining river or ocean streaming over our shiny coats and over our backs, feeling no readiness for and no anticipation of anything but what we can make flow by flowing ourselves through it. Like the war.

Like that. The chlorine fumes sting awake our noses, eyes, and tongues, and make us and the old girls look from the shallow end into the deep. The looking makes you drunk. You think you see yourself there in the blue pool where shadows stretch from trembling red ghosts, where blank bright mantas sail. Calmly falling to the bottom are ladders drawn in white crayon. Wavecups lift our reflected faces to us at a tilt.

When it is time, we swim.

On a dare he gave himself

Riddle: Once it was green and growing, now it is dead and singing.

He could tell everyone without them knowing in time.

He could find matches and get tinder along the way.

He could set afire the turning man-crow who scared him as a boy in the corn. (And who would that harm? Who would that harm?)

He could walk away from the waving man-crow's flames.

He could touch the flute tree from which so many were hewn.

He could remember "The Whole Chicken in the Soup." (And give every note the slip. Every single note.)

He could clear pretty Ann's stoop without snagging his heart upon thoughts of her cool arms and her lips and her darting tongue. (And who could that harm now she was gone?)

He could strip a jagged shingle from the eucalyptus she'd named Hag.

He could use it to rattle the brittle rose hips of her oldest Goldreds.

He could skip stones over dry riverbottom, hear the percussion of nine dry drums. (The sounds of falling. The failing sounds.)

He could dare himself to hear the chiff of the owlets under the bridge.

He could hear the huff of their mother's great wings folding.

He could be quiet for them, quieter than a hunted mouse.

He could balance himself on the high span's iron railings.

He could walk the whole length coming and going.

He could recall the riddle (and not an easy one): a final blessing.

Fiddle! he thought, and dared himself to lean out. And farther out.

19th & Minnesota

He was seeing things. His speech was incoherent. The spans, the beams, the eyebars of memory had weakened, and he had forgotten most of the crucial components of lying down, waking up, walking out, coming home. He and his grandchild wobbled up the street of cars parked nose-down by the tens of thousands, their auto-asses going right up the sky over The Bay. Tens and tens of thousands of hills, and, clearing the hilltops, throngs of dog-owners, two by two, holding Starbucks under their chins and bagged dog-shit mid-chest, short nylon leashes on their wrists. Broom-sweep gusts of wind made the pavement shimmers jitter and creased the dogs in their stylish coats.

When he saw, when she saw the cuffs of his pants float back, they both pitched forward. She felt and he thought a bird calling in the trees resembled something gone that had returned. He thought and she felt the sleepy drooliness of having a head as soft as the places upon which it rested.

She had just learned to walk. Without falling down, she polkaed the falling-down polka, feet and legs and arms and hands a bijection of X onto Y, an injection and a surjection where a surjection is any function whose domain is X and whose range is the whole of Y.

Brain-shocks and after-shocks had damaged his fluency in metamathematics, which had been his parents' language and, so, his own primary language from the beginning.

Nineteen months old, his grandchild spoke in word-murphs, word-blags, in drunken sentence-spooges.

He was dancing the dance she was dancing. He was seeing the things she was seeing, and when he said "only if" she said "if," and when he said, "For any number *n*, *n times zero equals*," she said, "Zzzero!" When she changed the flow of her breath between her tongue and palate, he felt his own flowing alter. They nailed the words zzzero and vvvvoom, every time, sustaining the v and z sounds insecticidally.

With no plan, they had become lost one step from her doorstep. Her mother and father had said to her and to her grandfather some words about not forgetting the bananas, and about remembering to be back for naptime. Their use of *and* and *not* had been, he felt, syncategorematic. Inside her nasal cavity, she smelled the word "annnddnnnodt." When it leaked out of her nose, it tasted potatoey. They had answered, "Vvoom," and after waving goodbye, hearing the door pull shut: "Vvvvoom!"

His son and his daughter-in-law called their five-block Dogpatch neighborhood "the nabe" because of the affection they felt for it. Elderly couples lived there. Young professional couples lived there, most of them with exactly two children. The grandfather thought of the place as a kind of ark. Ninety-eight years earlier, it had escaped the quake and fire during which so many had perished in clusters of buildings shaken down and incinerated like pine needles. I saw. Saw, and was the same. I asked nothing of the worlds I created, of the ones I destroyed. I valued them as neither possible nor necessary.

The grandfather had been told by his son there was a park within walking distance. Passing from not-q to not-p on the ultimate, changeless pavement, losing words and judgment in stillness and in movement, what he had taken in were the sounds *park, wind, walking, ants*. There were wide and narrow cracks in the sidewalk, and the wind multiplied zero in them with a sound like millet seeds raining. There were ants. Buffon ants, of the species Tetramorium caespitum. They could be placed at the entry point of a maze with 32,768 paths to a food source. They would formulate optimization algorithms, and, in only two efforts, they would locate it. The ants, the crumbs so slight the wind scuppered them.

His granddaughter explained: "Rrrrblurr hrrrblurrr hrrrbub capPOO."

He said, "Mmm-madda." What else to say, the shovel no tongue, the spout no mouth, the brain no faucet handle.

She led him to the car grilles she liked to touch on their damp noses, to pet and pal around with. There was no end to the car grilles. Up to the sky went they. Up to the sky.

He liked and she liked when the alarms went off, the cats-in-spandex sounds, the cause, somehow the cause of bursting-full flying words, day, toe, finger, pee, vvvvvery hubcap, hamstrings, earholes, ovvvvvvveralls, door, knob, knee-zzzipper. Belly bulging with belly-bay-bay-belly-bay. Vvvvvery bulging with possible banana.

He slowed down to unpeel hers.

He unpeeled his.

"BnnNNA! Loodofe loodofe," she said as she horned it against her face, her neck.

He pocketed the peels. "Loodofe," he said, left pocket. "Loodofe," he said, right pocket. He was, she was—because banana flesh and banana peel are perfection—thanking God.

I said, "You're welcome."

They budge-walked while they mashed the ban and the an and, finally, the na parts in their fists and ate from their palms. They smeared their fronts, their matching yellow pants, smeared the nose of one car named H, the nose of one named L, and one, 0000.

The passersby swayed a little on their leashes, their earbuds bowing their heads towards the heads of songs. They wore glasses or sunglasses, they wore hanging shit in shiny bags, they wore dogs, and their dogs looked up at the two, and plenitudes curved across their lenses. He was breaking stride with her. He was slowing down. And she.

And they. Were.

Slow.

With respect to time, their rate of change of angular displacement had shifted. With respect to location, their limbs had asked their muscles for help, and had received no answer.

After so much budging, they were suddenly unbudging.

Very still they stood.

Very still they stood.

He said, "Ah-hwooo. Hwooooo."

She could say the word "Yeah" and the word "Grandpa." Why say them? Her hand unthreading his finger in one turn, she said, "Hwooooo. Hwooo."
He said, "Hwooooo. Hwooo."
With great concentration, she said, "Hwooo. Hwoo."
Grandfather and grandchild having a bowel movement. Together. Formally, virtually, eminently satisfying.

God knows what the parents were thinking when they sent these two out to walk together, triggering the alarms of the resting cars, asking the calm blue old lady Mercedes about when the, how the, if the feeling of cooling comes in the face and the hood and the grille and the headlights where the best, hot, bright juices pour through.

The child watched the grandfather make the stink step, a way of lifting one foot and shaking lightly, the other a lighter shake and longer. She stink-stepped, too, a glance upward at him, a threading-in, an understanding: *We will be changed.*

I saw.
Saw, and was never the same. To be God and to not be them has caused me to offer this, my God resignation.
When I was alone with my omniscience, my satisfaction was absolute. My self-assured distance from the larger and the smaller humans

was so great that my acceptance of them was boundless. I felt they were facts, splendid facts. And my absolute closeness to them made it possible for me to *be* them, and to know they were not facts, not at all facts. Through eons upon eons: so many children holding one finger of the elder one and both of them pinballing around. I saw, and I did not miss a thing. And I was content in that condition.

I felt it was good to be God in the God garden, neither cast in nor cast out.

And then, these two came.

They were at quite a slant.

The hill was a steep one.

The question was: how to return home since down was good if you were sleepy, and, if you were sleepy, up was good?

He resented the sleepiness no less than she. A perfect mercy, sleepiness. A giant injustice.

His stomach and his brain rumbled. His innermost mouth recollected concepts it once could pronounce, the cap and cup of Boolean Algebra, the truth functors. His mind in his mouth remembered the search of pseudo-Boolean operators, which caused him to reach in his shirt pocket for it.

It had been there all along. He drew it out.

The rubber tongue.

In that same instant, her hand in his hand remembered that when one odd feeling tightened around another there was a tongue you could suck with your mouth and tongue. It had a nirvana handle.

· The pacifier.

He held the handle tightly. He took a hit, a hard hit. He had a selfish, ungrandfatherly impulse his love for her could not override.

Another hit of the pacifier. Hhu-uuuuh. Hhhu-uuuh.

Another.

She echoed back, Hhu-uuuuh. Hhhu-uuuh. Under the veil of her gaze she was a gristly, hungering young beast. With its paws and haunches pulsing. With the muscles surrounding its mouth rippling. With teeth. Able to grow more of them.

She made the verdictive sound: Uth.

Not, after all, wanting to bogart the smooth of the wet, pacifying spliff but already wanting it back, he gave her it.

Very lit, they swayed.

Very lit, they swayed.
Passing it back and forth.

Together, they said, "Sit," and at once crashed slowly down onto the pavement as they said it.

I asked, "*Here?*"

She nodded, an offer-answering, her tongue not entirely in her mouth. He offered me a place, the place between them where an intermediate conclusion could be placed.

I had made the world my body, mine alone. Humans lost it at the first hour of life and the last. Until then, the loss and the story of the loss mattered to me none at all.

Lying themselves down on, rubbing themselves into, moistening the pavement with the pigment of them. Curling up, forehead to forehead.

She pushed the rubber tongue into his hand. He pushed it into his mouth.

He gave it back. She put it in, but her own tongue, so thick with thistledown now, refused.

Trying to find his mouth, she nudged his cheek and chin with the pacifier handle. His scratchy neck, his nose.

His lips opened. The wind went in.

I saw. A toe-knock. A myoclonic stink-kick. A touch-landing sleep. A wings-retracting, membrane-thinning drowsing.

A sleeping.

The banana warming in his hair and hers. Ants swarming there.

Lattices of ants. Some of the car engines propellering, some of the front doors of houses making casking and uncasking sounds, tastes of fuel in the pavement shadows, seabed odors churning, leashes tacking, snapping, a dove sailing in, resting upon, rocking against timbers.

The nature of the business in Extraellaville

Drowned woman appears out of nowhere here in Extraellaville. Wet luggage. Mud on her, all dried. Three rings on her wedding-ring finger. Hair, with pierced clamshell pieces tied in, her whole rivery head tinkling. Jay and me got that close to her in our old Krispy Kreme Shell.

Nature of the business—nature of the business—snag what swims near the pumps—at the clean shore of the highway, at our rotting dock where you hang up, pay three bucks for our Premium.

"Shut *up!*" said Jay when he saw the stains under her breasts, stains on her undercups. Flower-print dress, almost transparent—half-slip—bed slippers silt-black, bless her, dead and clothed in dirt and some rose Goldreds.

"I want a cinnamon twist," she says, "want a coffee, want news of this world, got news of the next if you want, want revival folks who might want me, spirit come unto thee with not a penny—needed nothing once, asked for everything."

Not for one little minute did Jay or me wait.

I could be some wrong about that. We might've waited one minute—she wore those expensive shades she probably looted, spoke funny, was awful heavy—and wasn't she Jesusy as ever in that way me and Jay always hated.

Nature of the business is to offer service, no matter who washes in, wants thankless kindness, weak coffee, donuts that kill better than tanks. That's our religion, how we believe you know you're human.

Jar we had out nineteen years after our local girl went missing, jammed full of money just waiting one worthy cause. That was hers now—$111.11—bet that matters someway—five ones in a line.

Tears spill out from under her high-priced shades. She says, "Holy. Holy."

Drank coffee, and another, and another, thirsty, ate two more oily torpedoes, hungry so it broke our hearts to watch, took two triple-extra t-shirts we gave her, pulled them on over everything she wore.

129

We put her on the bus to Ellaville—it gasses up here—where our asylum set up rooms and jobs and meals and schooling for the incoming. But that sounds worse than it is. Our town gives what it can, and beyond our means.

"Live and let live" means nothing 'til you lost your daughter, 'til you waited nineteen years to hear her say what she wanted, restless—restless—our Ann, our big restless, trusting spirit always talking Jesus.

Our Ann.

Always telling us what she wanted next—was she different than any of us?

Used to say just that same way: Holy. Holy.

The story of their 67th

"Oh, it was—it was—am I right?—it was like you were at you were at you were in really in a movie—a big show a parade a fair a. Something." My mother touched flowers that were no longer around her neck.

"It was," Dad said. "It was like a—"

"—holiday or. Something." They were not there, the sweet-smelling garlands, but she touched them in a certain way, as if showing them to herself in that moment inside her when she and our Dad had gone on their anniversary cruise to Hawaii. They had planned it for at least twenty years. "Right off the plane—that fast—we got lei'd. I got lei'd in baggage—too hard to tell about—difficult difficult to describe—we kinda you kinda—bend—o-ver—"

"—bow—" Dad didn't seem to hear us all (except for the really oldest of the five of us, sixty-two now) snickering.

"—when they do you."

I used to be the teller of the family stories, before I destroyed my marriage to a person more worthy of my family's love than I. I have not forgotten the stories, not a single one, and they matter to me as much as ever. To the end of their lives, my parents were good people. They were not to blame that I am a man causing despair and shame in those who loved me.

She said, "It shakes you is what it does and you're not supposed to not allowed to it's you can't throw them away because it's—"

"—disrespectful—"

"—you're—you—what you do is when you get home you 'Return them to the earth.'"

"That's what they say."

"You put them back." She stretched out her legs. "You return them." She had on culottes. It's worth mentioning because she liked them. He liked them on her, and would say it within our hearing. Sitting close on the couch, he stretched his legs out next to hers, and you could make a fair guess they were once again sunk in deck chairs, they were becalmed under *The Eleanor Wilner Sovereign Class* bill caps issued to them, their exotic drinks and the sea-silence pleasing them.

She said, "They're a big people they're not a tall. People. Are they?"

"Nope. They're big around. Solid as salt licks."

Our parents could dance. In everything they did, they could find a common measure. Though her rhythm was always more broken than his, he could firmly guide and turn them. He could lead.

"*You*—you. It's like a—'salt licks'—really?—they're...what they're doing is piling on heaping on flowers and flowers—they're flowering you—are they?—how would you put it?—are they flowering you?—it's another world there and they put you really gently it's gentle it's gentle how they put you in it—it's an Island Life."

"Yeah. *Yeah*. You're somewhere out in the middle of nowhere, all right."

"It's something—every time it happens—it's—his was different than mine—mine—mine was all different in how it smelled how where how it—in the morning and at night—everything on you everything around you—it was fragrant. *God*. Fragrant like you just can't..."

"They come for you," he said.

Growing up and still feeling close, feeling together as a family, my sister and brothers and I had seen this at least ten-thousand strange times:

they were near enough for him to touch the back of his fingers against the base of her throat, for her to vine her fingers in his hands. "At the hotel lobby," he said. "They come right for you with those garlands. In the morning. The van. The restaurant. The pool. At night."

"Mmmmmmhm—mmmhmm," she said.

"With torches," he said.

I'll go home after this. Right after this. I promise.

This was 1993. If you split away from the world—if the world splits away from you—and it keeps returning to you as a Christmassy anecdote a long time later, you're going to want to tell it even if you never do remember it exactly right.

Thanks for letting me tell it.

Christmas Eve. The bar I was managing—this was in Tucson—was empty, so I had sent the bartender home. But two elderly women were there who wanted for me to acknowledge that they saw me poring over my errors in the books. They had toasted. They had picked up and put down their drinks and held hands on the tabletop and let their hands go. For nearly an hour it went on like that. Sometimes they glanced my way. I pored over the empty place—and over them. I figured they were about seventy years old or even a lot older. They were in party dresses, velvety red and redder velvety-red, and the dresses, lots of cleavage, were way too young for them. Well, that's what I thought. I was almost thirty, and I had the ideas a man has about old breasts. They look at you. They looked at me. I mean the women looked at me. I think they saw I was cleavage-watching, and I didn't—and I don't—think they minded. And finally we made eye contact. We hadn't made eye contact in all that time. Something barroom clever would follow, of course. There is time while you're drinking to figure out the clever things that are, in other circumstances, afterthought—am I right? They had touched arms and leaned shoulders in. At the time I would have called it "gag-worthy." They were all over each other. The effect was that their two old-lady perfumes fused and kind of scent-bombed the place. They were there—in the mushroom cloud of it. I was there. Nobody else was there. Something was going to be said, and it would be what is said in stories in bars, which are just about the only places where people can make every part of the story they're in. On a holiday in a bar empty except for the manager, people will exchange the gift of saying things that have been saved, that they can carefully package and offer to each other wrapped up the best they know how. I had observed that innocent effort. I had noticed how it feels so good to people to be un-awkward, they will want to let you listen in, as long as you stay behind the bar. You have to stay behind the bar. They brought their foreheads together. A kind of foreplay wattle-wobbling happened when they giggled.

They kissed.

God.

At the very same moment, their eyes closed. I pored over them. I don't believe they were making a show of it for me. I don't believe they had that need. I do believe it. I do believe it sometimes. It depends on how I am—and where. I hated them in so many ways. I hated them for no good reason, and the hatred doesn't seem to end. I closed my ledger. More of their touching. The contact of their pudding-flesh arms. Their mottled wrists and hands. The stink-cloud spreading. Lowering. An end of some kind was coming but coming in an old-ladies-getting-it-on-and-about-to-grind-it-oldstyle. I wanted for them to acknowledge that I closed my ledger because of them. The clever thing I offered was what I could offer. It was the perfectly predictable right thing to say, and better than "Merry Christmas." "Get a room," I said. They leaned back from each other. They separated, two not-so-tall-anymore candles burning at one table. I still haven't figured out how to describe it right, how to account for it.

It was like wind blew them hotter and brighter and almost out, but not. I listened to what they said to each other.

Thanks for letting me tell.

What did they say?

A lot of time has passed, but I'm pretty sure it was this.

"Forty years ago, she fell in love with me."

"I did. I fell hard."

"*Now* she tells me."

Shaken protest departure from local asylum

When will more arrive? we wondered, bunked everywhere on the five floors of The Home, which is the local asylum. And then last week we were shaken into The Population. Yes, *shaken* is what they called it.

And they put me with an old woman like me: a person named Them. Aide said, "Them's tri-polar, Ann," warned me Them might do, say, desire three things at the same time. "Ignore Them is your best, safest policy," said Aide.

And, "You can ask her her name, but, you know, you know it." The room and quarter of a bathroom was better than three days in a line, than two square feet of stadium, than a poison homecoming. Had curtains.

Had fresh linens.

Had half of a closet.

My life could be shaken into this room: a bug let out of a paper bag. Don't think I'm not grateful. I am. "You incurable?" Them asked, adjusting our ceiling set. That was first. Second, she grinned.

She grinned, muted it, said, "You drowned," and, third, changed the volume bar, you know that bar appearing over the TV faces? And decided that a volume of 26 was about right, that's two buttonpushes past the bar's midpoint.

She said, "There's a lot of us in the lost jar."

I said, "There is."

There is. Holy. Holy.

The backless gowns, the rhythm of night rounds, the meal and shower and recreation and therapy schedules, the locked boxes over the phones and fire axes, the visiting hours, the van into and back from downtown: it's fine.

Especially for those of us over seventy, The Home is our home now.

It is our place in The Population.

It is our nation whole.

Them and me go to the Injuring Clinic on Monday mornings, popular with the undammed who washed up here in Ellaville like good delta silt, and who wanted to hurt more than we already do for what we left.

Them, who understands better than anyone, won't leave her loaner iPod alone, and has tried to teach me the thrashing thing iPodders do in the commercials, those hot white earwires whipping around them, their shoe tongues out.

Their clothes flapping up or down or off. ("That's some fun," my stepfather used to say after a bath with my disgusting stepmother.) Them could break or dislocate her hip without ever falling, dancing like that, like on a skillet.

You bring two empty tube socks on Monday, one to hold the harder punishments, one for the softer, and you don't hurt each other at first, it's pretend, it's a comic routine at first, like you don't mean it, like you're—what?

Like you're hitting rubber nails into rubber boards with rubber ball-peens. Then, Them will swing the sock with coffee beans in it hard against your cheek, and there's the brewed, breakfasty, pleasant Monday morning smell.

And Them—not at all a stranger, Them, a violent joy, Them, your personal revenging angel—strikes you good, and again. And comes the asterisked visions, comes the screeching violins swelling, the orchestral bruising.

Comes the stinging tear-spilling. And, after a while, a fine rouge of coffee powder on your cheek and jaw. And, after a while longer, a stimulating cloud that the loaded sock flies through to have one blasting last whack at you.

This, all of this, costs nothing. It is at the taxpayer's expense. I was unshaken all my life into The Population, had strange-good family, lifelostlong friends, three husbands, two children-ruins I outlived in a parish I loved like a hundred-year flood.

Never had a companion good as Them.

She tells me she will kill herself if I stay.

She tells me she will do it sooner if I go.

Visiting privileges at Les Gauld Motors, downtown Ellaville

If you bring it in for balance, you must believe. When you bring it in for timing, for less left-tilting, for the scraping sound first thing in the morning, for underperforming, overheating, you must believe.

When you return Chito's phone call, always call his cell, because sometimes he's test-driving your car, out burning rubber for the sake of the accelerator or to test your brakes, or he's making love in order to calibrate the buck in your bucket seats, or he's joy-riding with different degrees of joy just to see, just to see.

Used to be he brought me.

Now, he always picks up our boy Joe along the way to pulling down into a dry arroyo; and, above the sound of the crunching undercarriage, Chito might say to Joe, "A freezing problem with this one" or "Lady says the engine makes a sorrowing sound."

You can call, and Chito will put Joe on, so his five-year-old echo can say something diagnostic, Chito in the background whispering, "Tell her these Sadness Engines're stubborn"—"Tell her about our special on anti-antifreeze"—"Say we got us a gunning situation"—and Chito roaring, laughing—and then the engine and the boy and the back and rear bumpers all ripping hell or heaven open as if your car, thoroughly test-shaken, checked body and chassis, was at the quiet intersection of Repair & Destruction, the cell signal breaking, all-of-a-mysterious-sudden not reaching the there wherever Chito and Joe are or were.

You must believe.

You'll get it back in one piece almost and you'll feel a strong pull dangerously left or right, hear a spectral valve rattle, smell a croupy insuck of air, the stick fouled up, too loose, too free, the tank empty, oil low or out, everything gummed up and grinding, the rear end swaying sickly, the shocks—what shocks?—the brakes—what brakes?—nothing, nothing, *nothing* fixed.

Not the car, the boy, the man. Nothing that a warranty covers, no matter the miles. Chito will say, "Did I mention labor?" if you dare mention the cost of parts.

I left Chito when Joe was born—only choice I had. He got his and I, mine. No lawyers and no tears, not many. And mercifully friendly. But. Still.

But I still take mine in to him—feels like the thing to do. I call Chito's cell to hear what our son, happy as gasoline, will say, who has no real idea, the little cruiser, our boy, who can't even see over the dash, or reach the brakes or gas pedal, guided and powered by his misguided dad, our little piston dressed in his small mechanic's jumper that Chito's mom made him out of chamois.

I call to hear Joe, but also Chito, hiccup-laughing hard, whispering, and Joe imitating, already skilled at that mechanic's drawl, "You got you a—well—we call it—a Menstrual Pressure difficulty"— "What you need is—you need a rebuilt Peterbilt."

Things like that are the whole what and why of how I left, and things like that are the reasons I stay here in Ellaville for the continuing corruption of my son.

Imagine: a mother condoning such awful influence on him, a boy taken for a test ride by his father, wild behind the wheel of someone else's transportation—my son who can rinse his own plate, fold his own clothes, put them on hangers, in drawers, straighten his room and neatly make his bed, say his night prayers, and who prays, "I want to see my dad, God—he makes me scared."

Greetings from Teacher Reptile on the occasion of Father's Day and the publication of the final volume of *The Wrath* septology

And when the six thunders had uttered their voices, I was to write the seventh. I heard a voice from heaven saying unto me, "Teacher Reptile, seal up those things which the six thunders hath uttered and shred not the 7-set."

Upon the curbs and banks of the kinked firmaments, my wheels I kicked: Seekaa. Seekaaa-aaa-aa.

I went to the angel, which had the trumpet, and to whom was given the golden altar, and I said unto him, "Dirtpile me the advance for the seventh vial of *Wrath* to pour upon the dag, the chode, the donut shop, the BGP, the BGL, the betty and the barrel." I said unto him, "Serial me the seventh, Servant Abaddon, give unto me the great chain, that I may rule the pit without bottom, the session that hath not end of grind."

And so spoketh my angel servant, "It is done. Though your front truck take lip, ledge, coping, rail, ye shall not be schralped, no ass knife shall cometh nor letter in the mailbox." He said unto me, "Take it up and eat it. And it shall be hammer, banger and radical; and in thy mouth ill diamondz sweet as honey. And righteous airfeet you shall ollie."

"This you have carried to me from the sealed chambers?" I asked. "This you have delivered from the eternal?"

His eyes chrysolite, the angel servant's understanding reaching beyond the cunning thermal, he said, "It is done, Father Teacher Reptile Master. It is done."

The habitation of, the hold of, and the hateful cage of, the mellow varial and bitter belly of wrath I have madeth for them, for readers grommet and juvenile, for pavement kickers global madeth I the 6,156 pages in seven print and seven vook volumes, 77 translations worldwide, 76 movie hours, Teacher Reptile 1067th richest earth-person, 16 degrees honorary, commencings 7, medals conferred by President Hawaiian Christ-thorn Muezzin. Let him that hath understanding count the number, for it is the number of a man.

From the womb was I delivered to the cauldron; in the cauldron was my meat simmered down so that even as an infant I became boiled root, ribbed leather handle, maw tipping a rope of gristle. Except that I was formed thus how could I have been else than Serpent Convict Alpha Icon Literary, more Father to your child than Dad and Grandad, more real than God spiritual, their holiest home-school mentor? How am Teacher Reptile the author of your children's rapture, how am I in their every aciddrop tech dog skater dream? How do they hear the sound of my K-grind and hard pop?

Seek. Seek. Seekaaa.

I was immaculate conceived for devising and publishing the six hells. Myself a seventh now have made steezy. And live there no longer, and tomorrow return to prison. (Author fathers, I advise against tapping criminally those who have you criminally tapped.) There, in the stall that has often been my tranny funbox home, my consecutive sentences will be maximum: the next multi-volume phenomenon will I begin. And your ripening clusters of skater children I will once more delam who have in Christian cribs instead of cauldrons grown, have human been

and raised, have had fathering to make of them wheelbiters
of loathing. And, lo, my books and the concordances for and
dictionaries of they will love against your helpless rage. You
from whose ooze I have formed my testimony cannot halt them
entering my serpent mouth, open book of six-hundred-threescore-
and-six abominations.

My own father off-fucked at my birth, my mother a nussed,
hamburgered piss-pedaler, living dead girl on-the-hook street
pusher, bailed, mongo, brought me trashed boardbeast the first at
six, my papaboard. And brought me the second scud at nine, and
beastdaddy the third at eleven. And at eleven sold me by the hour,
the nOOb fruit she could bring to the poser saved who savored
that darkslide. The same, the same helped her return me when to
lesser hells I ran. After partaking of me and her, the same
pastor devourer prayed over child and mother.

Bless us, O Lord, for these thy poisons that answer the prayers of
the child learning murder. On my birth-morning twelfth that was
her last, I asked her would she go with me to the lot to check my
one mad skill. She brought the pastor who dealt us as a pair. She
watched. She had never seen.

"What is that?" she asked me, her son, bait, juicy steak. "What is
that where you go up and...?" And she and pastor wolf-laughing
howled when I told them.

"Ollie. Tic Tac. Nollie."

Later in that morning cameth I to she who pierceth me and cause
me to wail. I fed the mother serpent the last portion.

Her eyes like unto the furnaces of torment she showeth me them the light eaten out, and I saw her suspect, no grindage, trick-sketchy, mobbed, plagued-mad and hamster-fetus homeless dead by my twelfth.

After the nose bonk, the sack-it focus, cometh the blunt. After the snakerun rail cometh the o-vert, the air boneless.

Out of my mouth into her grave goeth a sharp sword: "The great whore has fallen and is reaped and has borne into revert the voice with the seven horns, the seven heads, the seven plagues of hail, the clouds of locusts the shape of seven black tongues."

New Year's Eve, my brother monk, eleven miles apart from me, in his thirty-second year at Lady Mori's Garden Soto Zen Temple in Wendellton, North Carolina, sends annual text, "How was 2014?"

I put on my dance shoes—yes, I have dance shoes!—and nearly every week of 2014, I shag-danced with my sweetheart—she has dance shoes too!—our soles are smooth, made for shuffling back and forward and falling and finding sureness, made for pivoting—

in a lowdown just-off-the-highway bar—with friends who share our love of James Brown singing Joni Mitchell ("How Do You Stop?") just for us, the dancers, our friends—dancing Blue Ridge friends dipping their toes in the dance floor talcum patch to get that chalkboard-cursive effect—and she & I half-hooking and hauling each other out of The Basic and into The Catch and out of The Catch into The Roll-Out—

and I'm supposed to lead—I have dance shoes! She has dance shoes!—

Is leading ever truly impossible in dance shoes?—

I'm supposed to lead or create the illusion of leading—(illusion achieved off tempo: I believe I might be made for exactly this)—and she asks, "Try a Sugar Foot? Try a Sugar Slide? Butt Roll? Applejack? Walk Back? Tuck Turn? Hesitation?"—

nearly every week, my sweetheart & I dance in this dicey, dimly lit place of sticky walls and bad acoustics that is shaggy late-middle-age where there is a crack in the concrete dance floor, a danger reminder that you can damage yourself permanently on Muddy Waters' "Blow Wind Blow"—

"Slip-and-Slide? Groove? Cruise? Shoulder-Drape?" she asks, trying for that mirror-step, offering me bring-it-on eye contact— and I have left my glasses on the table next to my sweating bottle of Corona and that is—isn't it?—a symbol of thirsting and insight (or blindness and fulfillment)—at last reconciled—

there is an electric bull ride in the bar and, only petting the bull, gently, every week, I am glad there is the damaged-looking mirror-mounting but no mirror in the cave-like men's room where not every week but surprisingly often one or more of us practices syncopated foot movements at the urinal—

I wipe down my dance shoes after Etta's "Love and Happiness" and BB's "Never Make Your Move Too Soon," while The Temptations are singing, *"I'm ready to surrender, my love"*—

"Whoahwhoahwhoah-oh!" I whisper-wail inside the echo of *"I've waited for this moment, my love"*—she is unshoeing and singing too, "Whoawhoahwhoah-oh!"—all of that leaving every week and every week returning with my sweetheart feels like dancing, like seeking, almost finding, seeking the beat

—then we are shod in our so-called normal life and rising up to our full heights and wavering because another shadow-dispelling song is pulling at us as we stroll out holding hands, dance shoes swinging in our other hands.

When I would take it from him there was the problem

When I would take it from him there was the problem of
backwash—his backwash not mine I mean since I took from
the bottle but didn't give back the way my brother did—lots of
brother-pitch lots of brother-molasses—so much there was a fizz
recarbonating the soda and so much the drink didn't absorb the
gob—and I would want to give it a shake or a stir just to cope
with the added value but I didn't I could've but didn't—"No
prob" he would have said if he noticed and I know he mostly
noticed because he would grin when I stared and gulped or
gulped and stared or winced and swallowed—he could've stopped
of course I could've started backwashing in order to make it
fair—he could've got his own bottle and I would've got mine no
prob no prob never was but we couldn't've wouldn't've I guess
and kept making spit brew with it going to him first and then
me—and why that order—younger to older—who knows—and
the last gulp never mine because he took it from me and drank
it down leaving some in there but not enough to pass on. Except
now now—now when I'm about to make a purchase—something
I plan to send to him but then keep for myself—I know I would
take that gulp from him though it smelled like fresh bootshit or
old stinkbait—no prob at all I would take it from him and look
where I could put some of my own in—and tilt it up toward
him—then give a toast—Here's to you brother—and tilt it back.

Hitchhiker, Seedvul, North Carolina, asked by the driver,
"Where to?"

The driver reminded me of you.

You broke my thumb. Twice. I remember that sometimes,
Brother. All my fingers blue-black. Then orange. Green. I couldn't
hold a spoon good because I was not a lefty—so: food on me for
sixteen weeks. We both thought it was uncanny that you could
do that with one spinning bullet basketball pass. I should have
seen it coming. And it happened again almost as soon as the
styrofoam-lined metal hand brace came off. You should have
seen it coming when you shot with the same speed as ever at my
hands, unopened and held out. And then, another metal brace
holding my thumb away from me. What in hell was I thinking?
What were you?

Wendellton would be good. Could you leave me there?

Bright-Very

It is all I ask. The stiff collar, stylish collar, the shirt color called *Bright-Very*, perfect fit, button-down, no busy pattern drawing undue attention. It dresses up and dresses down, easy-iron, masculine.

I feel it compensates for my impotence. I feel it fully compensates.

My loves, I cannot bring you—or me—to life with this body.

Bury me in this.

The color in the bed of the river? You wonder, **What is it?**

It kills me.

I have a heart murmur. I wish it would stop.

Still, I listen.

See. It's the fall leaves.

You are the best audience we have ever had.

You are. And tonight your eyes threw shining coins at each other and us. And we felt the showering goodness bring us down from our wire. We flew up on the next tune. We fell back down on the spines of our refrains. This'll be this'll be this'll be me, we sang on the bridge, on the fiddle bow we drew across each other. At one time, we were all three in love with pretty Molly and Sarah-Jane in the city, Rose and Lucy and Miss Lydia in the country, and in the mountain folds of our dreams, June Carter. None like her. June Carter, June Carter, this'll be me, sweet singer, this'll be me. We sang at the hand-hewn door to be let in Christmas Eve, at the head of the key in the prommed-up high school gym, at the too-young-to-be-married wedding receptions of some of our crushes, at the Mt. Mitchell Ranger Station parking lot because our instruments were in the van and who would stop us, and at that Krispy Kreme in Extraellaville for the lost girl who was never found but came back on her own. Years and years later. Pretty Ann. Pretty Ann in the asylum, this'll be this'll be this'll be me, we sang on the courthouse steps for a return engagement on July fourth in Extraellaville.

Two bars into the second piece in our set, a hippie in the audience shouted out that there was a song about the last leviathan, did we know that one—and started singing in the middle of our tune, interrupting us but probably too stoned to have tracked that, she sang, a ring of hearers forming around her, we ploughed on, the idea of a band is to set out and not sail back, her ring of listeners widening, the span of it growing, the depth, and her focus, it was total focus, she had words to the song, she was singing words but they were whale-sounds, the last calling of the last whale alone, when whales still were around and were flying seadrums in pods with their reverb up beyond max, she was like the National

Geographic recordings of them, a solo whale could sound everything in and on the underwater mountains and plains, it was a pretty great thing, good that we have the recordings, and we quit playing in order to let her go on, she was going in so far, one of those hippies eighty or more years old that come right out of the earth, you see more and more of them if you're a musician with the dirt and desire still on you, and you recognize that they have mud and want still on them, faces and arms and legs and clothes mottled where rain hit the dust on their skin and splashed and crusted when they ran for shelter from it, you notice that sometimes they are wearing WalMart reflective vests over their hippie stuff, or they have a Burger King crown on, disco wands on necklace strings hang from their necks, this was a long song with between-the-phrases silences, the silences that come after leviathans that were there but are gone.

After a while it felt right to join her, to join in, like she had thought and everyone there had thought we were dead, but we returned to back her, sounding quiet as shut schoolbooks, we backed her wailing, well, there is not a better word for it, she was wailing, if you have known an old human that everyone agrees has something real wrong with her because she is more like a young bear or wet, stumbling deer or unweaned weasel or newborn bee than a boy or a girl, you have hoped they could come from where they have been and be human—but why wish for that, why if she can sing like no human anywhere?

You are. You are the best audience we have ever had.

Except for that audience for the hippie woman. They were better than you, to tell the truth. We were on a tour. It was what we

153

called "our tour" though that wasn't at all honest. We asked her to come along. She didn't. We didn't ask twice. She wouldn't have survived the road real. You had to be real road to survive the road real. We were paid in food and beer, a place to sleep sometimes, cash enough for gas and van repairs. At The Grand Closing for a deadly hot springs that killed over twenty in two year's time, we sang for sixty dollars in goods at the town's True Value Hardware. We split that between us on different things but bought six rolls of duct tape for the common good. We have moved on. There are no small towns like other small towns. All small towns are unlike the places you dream you will go to. This'll be me, this'll be me, this'll be, this'll be. We never will know anything like you.

And after these cries, I, Teacher Reptile, heard a dementer on the bank say to me from the lake of fire, "This is the second death" and "Here there shall be more pain"

and "Here more pain and sorrow where the former torments are passed away," and "This is the first book."

His raiments shone like unto an apostle of the Lamb, and he said unto me, "Write. The fountain will flow freely."

He who was bloodkindred old school gave me roll-in. *Uncle* the suit called himself whose gate made the sound of feeblegrind— and I was fear-singing against it—and whose white car crossed the signs of warning—and in that car I was hissing my brain's shove-its and popshove-its of self-losing—while I was thrashing through my fears' waxmarks and thrilled by the passages of thrashing—and his headlights halogened the cyclone security beam flooding above—and during all that driving I was in the open mouth of my own instrument, I was storying the other coming towards, and I was in and through the pipe—then miles of woods private—I was storying the other leaving, in the sealed upholstered Cadillac chamber where I was my own arriving first sound. And the tires crunched the steep traverses up. And through an iron arch came I to his home, and he took me into a wing.

And inside, another wonder: a room he said was mine.

He called it mine, my Uncle tapping my back so that my body drew in the stars of heaven where storying, storying, storying, my mind had brought forth the little cell. I had framed it up, the room, my room, mine, and I had furnished it, gave it the scritching wall-shadows and the closed-door closet of, the rattling windows of, the revolving milling floor and countervailing ceiling-fan of a father's voice.

And Uncle gave me keys, my own, and, he said I could climb
in, and I did without undressing even my feet, the metal teeth
of the things still in my fist, I was, was I asleep already when he
said—he could not have—could not have—he said, his starry tie
swinging, its trillion soothing tips brushing me—"There is in the
seven-story tunnel under your room, a vast realm, and with these
keys you will go down." And he left. The closing door clicked.

I put the seven keys to my lips, and sucked each one.

The next life. Mine in the storying, already mine.

From that hour, the tree of life, which bear seven manner of
fruit, yielded its fruits. I had table, board, food, board, bed,
board, friends technical. Every several gate was of one pearl, each
pearl full of eyes within: *the books*. The books—the books!—the
dream-ramps, the books, the brain-noggles, the books like
daddy-lap, daddy-arms the books, the airwalk grabs—the books
and the books!—the paradises of sets to bust. The books the
torpedo-quiet when-you're-sleeping kisses. The splenic traumas
leaping in, leaping out louder than bombs, the hunting-for-me
books, the blood-on-their jowls books. They opened unto me the
strangeways, the garageland.

Seekaaa. Seekaaa. Seekaaaaaaa.

Then Uncle, mother's tricktionary John, he street-oil-sub-baron,
said, "Give me the little volume of my own account so I may open
the purse that openeth and no man shutteth."

And came the Godhound buses and in them friends, Ams upon

Ams in throngs, their boards embracing, hips and shoulders winding, arms in the aisles, hands gliding the floor, pickin up change.

At Magogwrath Academy were my pages turned; at Gogwrath were they become transparent glass. Here, said they, the 360, here the 180, the boogie, the 50-50. Look, said they who saw how my heart faced left, look, said they, a goofy-foot yob. And they judged me not, put me vert, poured in idea gasoline. Here is more, said they, as were I their son.

Seekaaa—aaa-aa! Seeekaaa!

What city is like unto this great city!

What righteous citizens! VFM, Uke, Ask Panic, Morris, Shank, Sheila Remoan, Click Track, Hey This, Synth, Suffer, Pizzle, Crap Cut. We nicked our names from Clash and Smiths, we were live show and hollow hatful, skating shibby through pipe and inside concrete empty gut and the combat way out.

We called the lifting 'ticketing' and did it slappy, fakie, tweaked the method, and retweaked.

And I and my tribe overcometh the learning wall great and high, we openeth the twelve gates, our names written thereon, on the east three gates, on the north three gates, on the south three gates, and on the west three. "Dropping!" we cried nailing hip ollie, dog piss, Christ air, Bigspin, Casperflip.

"Dropping! Dropping! Dropping!"

Burly, we departed from that holy city that lieth foursquare, the length as large as the breadth.

Bless us, O Lord, for these thy holy cities of freedom. Bless us for thy prisons in which Teacher Reptile has incarcerated been and in which, at nineteen, all seven of his volumes he outlined in his first four hours of cell-time. Bless us for the nine-year first fraud conviction, and for the release from prison at twenty-eight. Bless us for the seven *Wraths* visited upon the world in the sixteen rapturing years following. For the old crimes, the incorrigible new, for the second sentence, the second verdict, for the beginning of the long-term without-parole time federal, bless us. Bless us for the return to prison until the Teacher Reptile shall be not less than one hundred and four.

For my kindling is the world border to border, noble barn to noble barn, and I have set afire the amazons and the paper-millions. Wrath-fires I have madeth for the Bible-clinging hands. And produced them bigger Wrath volume greater, longer and more fundamental as they have grown older. And made each book a closer as their minds have sealed closed. The Wrathmore website, launched sacred-glue-psychotic two-oh-one-two, reveals, quoth webwrathmaster, "Teacher Reptile is the only band that matters, the writer for all ages evo-delusional developmentally arrested cometh he, and for their unsaved fathers. Unquietly he cometh. And quickly."

Seekaa. Seekaa. Seekseek. Seekseek. Seekseek. Seekseek. Seekaaa.

Perfumery

for S.B.

An upended bell. Not struck, but touched awake.

"We call this place The Pair-foom-airy," said The Perfumer.

"When did I arrive here?" he asked and, to please her, "Here at the pair-foom-airy?" It was just like him to ask last questions first. Because: where he was he was, as if what he was was the perpetual is, the is that shall have felt, felt, feels as infinite as the exquisite dark-defeating seedling-green skin of the unclothed voluptuous Perfumer.

He asked, "Are you? Actually? Green?"

He asked, "And have we always met?" and "Am I ever awake?"

She whispered back, "Yes I am we have we shall have. You are. You are awakening now."

He looked around, slow shaking of his head, and then his shrug, his grin, and said, "This place is small."

The Perfumery was smaller than a rowboat stood on its stern. Smaller than the bathroom on an airplane. A spirit there could row some, fly some, take to the sky or to the sea.

The Perfumer's body was so close to his that her knee pressed his knee when she kicked at the pearl-shell gown pooled around his feet as if a former self.

And he heard the bell, from behind. Or.

Or both within and behind him: radiating.

If her sun-suffused jade face, jade eyes and brows were less close, he might not have grinned and said, "I'm here! I'm in The Perfumery!"

"Pair-foom-airy," she said, her forehead brushing his, sweet orange, clary sage, valerian, her tossed-up hair imprinting its chrism there, lovage, marjoram, labdanum, her knee pressing once more, and then.

And then withdrawing, the afterfragrances neither there nor disappearing.

159

"The first," she said, and when his laughter robed them in the little booth, she touched her fingertips upon the light scarves of laughter at her throat, and then at his, and up to his ear, the cartilage and thin glove of flesh there.

And behind his ear, her fingers, her fingers, laurel, anise, ambergris, her hand opened, the soft back of her hand moved across and down, the camphor of her hand, and caressed, in passing, his warming nipples.

She leaned in to move her neck against the pulsepoint in his. Up. Up.

Her lunar cheek and chin vined his chin and cheek, two different resins perfuming him, under, against his earlobe, her hand closing upon his chest.

"Is that," he said, "my heart?" He meant, That bell—that bell.

She said, "My hand."

"My heart," he said.

She said, "Perfumed," pressing harder, and releasing her fist. "The second," she said who would be numberless in her gifts. Where her head and her hand had been, he felt incensed, and said, "I'll burn here!" but she was closer, consoling, they were as close in this deep, narrow space as two embracing mists.

And he thought that he had only thought, Is this what I wished?

She said, "Yes."

Clearing silence followed and burning closeness as her breasts and belly murmured him.

He heard the bell's echoing oblations lifting from their crib of sound, the chording of the world coming in and leaving.

And returning.

"Am I the cause?" he asked, who eternally was.

Garlanding him in her arms, she smiled, said, "Turn," and meant "Around."

He obliged. She orbited him, his chest pricked by her aureoles, his belly astringent against hers. The circumscenting friction of their contact wound him, them, him, her, him, them in shrouds of scourging pleasure.

Inside her arms, he turned.

"The third," she said, but hadn't there been many perfumings in the moments, and an eternity of moments more than three?

Turning within the bowl she made of herself, he sounded her, he sounded his own skin, he created a gleaming, ringing sound in The Perfumery. And beyond.

Not struck but touched awake from these dreams of you, I thought I could not, could not bear your death.

I thought—how foolishly I thought!—I could not give you up even to The Perfumer, the fragrant earth, dear friend.

You want to know—

—why I hate you.

It's that you no longer let me learn my way over you, my singular chronic harassment, my particular persistent curse. You no longer let me lay my eggs like a louse in your pulse, traveling, unwelcomed, with you everywhere around and also far from this filling station in Extraellaville.

Me, the cause of your tics, dear Jay, the mite skating over your eyemeat, blade-blade—glide-blade-blade.

It's a wonder I never came off in the wash or here at our workplace or from your unnatural hairpiece. Have I ever mentioned this: how I hated nothing about you—not the back rash, not the butt lint, not the rubber-black rug riding low on your forehead? As if you could cover what had recessed and recessed and been replaced by bald folds (practically flaps) of something I never once saw as ugliness.

Buy a ball cap, would you?

If you won't let me back into that face, if you won't put me under your gaze again, I will hate you today all day. I'm going to have to. I'm going to have to.

I don't like to—I didn't say that I want to.

But, dear dearest, dear, dearest dear Jay, how I used to go figure-eighting over your skin right after we swam (Remember? We had Special Permission!) in that not-crystal-clear pool at the Ellaville Inn with the dog turds on the bottom. You said, "Helluva thing to do to a dog," and I said, "Better than the hot tub."

(The turds were calm in their place. They were not crumbling. At the time, that was important to us.)

(Five of them in a mysterious formation.)

You said, "Large."

I said, "Animal," I said, "Magnified by eight feet of water." I said,

"No turbulence."

We were more or less weightless, our arms were wings going out and in through the water, our legs and feet bicycling the evening light. That was a good day all day.

And I moved in on you—this was before you were a cheating shit that I hate—and you moved in, too, and liked it, admit it.

You swam down because I asked you to, it seemed like I could ask anything, and you went down, went down, came up gasping. You confirmed it:

Crap.

Laughing bounces beautiful off water, doesn't it?

I asked, "Fresh?

You asked, "Do you gotta know?"

And went down, down, down for me. That was, it was, it was a good day. That was a good day.

And right then, that same evening, a dog that you said looked like Oprah in the days before fame, a dog, a Skye Terrier, danced onto the pool diving board. And bounced. Five bounces.

An agile Skye Terrier. Graceful. And looked at the two of us as if we were the most lovely humans it had ever seen being. And dove headfirst.

That was amazing, wasn't it?

"You're so pretty!" the Skye Terrier said, pawing up onto the pool ladder, shivering off the green and goldredrosy water. Five more bounces, and it dove.

That was in the days before The Oprah Empire, when O was in the same pool, so to speak, as we were, except she was on television and already losing that shaggy Chicago look, and nowhere near the Gauld Apartments across from Les Gauld Motors. That was years before we lost our daughter.

Our walls were chlorine green, our floors, our ceiling, our light fixtures, mini-refrigerator, pillow shams—the sheets were. All the bedding.

I said, "Even the water coming out of the shower!"
You said, "Even the sinks!"

All day that day I didn't once hate you.

Aisle 4, Mini Bob's Mart

"Should we get a pumpkin? They're marked down," said Kay.
Kurt said, "We should have a cart."
"They're marked down—like I said."
Kurt asked, "Ever buy creamed corn?"

"Okay," said Kay, "let's get a cart."

The P.A. crackled. Customers! All pumpkins, *all* pumpkins
marked down.

"Oh, Kay," said Kurt, "let's have a cart. A big cart, a great cart—
the biggest we can have. With crazy wheels."

"But not too soft," said Kay.

"I love you, Kay. *That one? Pretty soft. Let's weigh it.* I always have
loved you. Always. *Are you sure?*"

"It won't cost much."

for Russell Edson

Batter

Sometimes the man spits before he grips. Sometimes bat & man
have a little chat, him choking up a bit to get the sense of the
meat, saying, *Where I want it now, Mister—straight shot.* He
knows it never hurts to practice-swing, to pound the plate, to
chop from the chin, from the gut, from the hip, to imagine the
crack-sound, to knock the thing against his thighs, rap it against
his lifted cleats, hold it up as if to switch on the ballfield lights
with it. He might dirt his palms and sand the wood with a
milking stroke, check whether he holds it hard-viced. For good
luck, he might kiss the head, butt, sweet spot, but, in any case,
not more than one kiss. One is the sum of what The Diamond
desires. One extra will curse the whole stadium. None is wrong
if other men are on base. He touches bill, bat, touches cup,
bat, touches ass, bat, smells, touches bat: in that order only.
The balance is the matter, not the heft, not the weight. If only
joined to the grain of his mind, a man takes it in his hands,
pulls the curving planet toward him, sends it complete to the
beyond—and not the great beyond, because, of course, he knows
the batter must feel greatness, feeling that fire is a batter's stance.
Ask him if it is, he will say, "Natch," trusting the matchstick itself
to know how shallow or how deep, how blunt or how precise it
should strike to get him home. He understands that of all blisses
this one lasts the least in time. And now his shoulders, arms, his
hands forget, remember, now the whole of him regrets the team.
He wants apartness, absolute aloneness, the grunt of contact, the
launch, the release.

I apologize to those in hell for my disturbances.

(Robert Bly, "Monet's Haystacks")

Glossary, the Teacher Reptile tales

50-50: fifty-fifty; type of grind; grinding with the axles of both trucks on the edge of the object

180: one-eighty; rotation of one hundred and eighty degrees

360: three-sixty; rotation of three hundred and sixty degrees

Aciddrop: skating off the end of an object while ollieing or touching hands on the board

Airfeet: when the skater's feet come completely off the board

Airwalk grab: in the air, grabbing the nose while the front foot is kicked out and the back foot is kicked back so they are in a walking type position

Am: amateur

Ass-knife: board stuck in the butt

Bail: to fall; while in the air, kicking the board away for a painless landing

Banger: excellent trick

Barrel: a fat girl

Betty: extremely hot girl

BGL: Background Loser

BGP: Background Props

Bigspin: 360-degree shove-it

Blunt: up over an object

Boneless: skater's hand removed from the board before landing

BSTL: Balls Stuck to Legs.

Burly: big trick involving potential for pain

Casperflip: board flipped, caught upside down, flipped over, spun backside 180 on its vertical axis, all while in the air

Chode: insult; pronounced cho-duh; crusty piece of poop on your butt

Christ air: crucifix position; holding the board out to one side

Dag: can mean anything; as in, "Dag, that was sweet!"

Darkslide: slide in which the board is flipped for half a kickflip, then caught with the back foot on the darkside of the tail and the front foot on the darkside of the nose and brought down by the skater into a slide on the middle of the griptaped side of the deck

Delam: abbreviation, delamination; the deck of the board becomes chipped, peeled

Diamondz: perfectly executed trick

Dirtpile: dirtpiling, doing something forbidden

Dog piss: dogpissing; skater grabs mute right by his front foot and kicks off his back foot as if a dog taking a piss

Donut shop: cops

Dropping!: yelled to prevent a collision as a skater drops into a section of a skate park

Fakie: travelling backwards

Feeblegrind: grinding with the front truck over the top of the object

Focus: to snap a board into two pieces

Funbox: street course with grindable and slideable surfaces

Goofy-foot: facing left, pushing off with left foot

Grind: any variety of trick in which the hanger of the truck grinds along the edge of an obstacle

Grindage: good food

Grommet: Grom; little kid skater

Hamburger: serious scrapes and cuts

Hammer: excellent trick

Hamster-fetus: synonym for fucked-up person

Hesh skater: an 80s-style skater.

K-grind: crooked grind; grinding along on the leading truck without having the board over the object

Kinked: as in kinked rail; a 2-kink or 3-kink rail increases difficulty

Letter in the mailbox: really bad wedgie

Mobbed: description of a not-so-great trick

Mongo: pushing mongo; skater uses his leading foot, the incorrect one, to push

nOOb: newbie

Noggled: being hit in the nuts by the board.

Nollie: an ollie off the nose of the board rather than the tail

Nose bonk: a very short nose grind involving a quick bonk of the front truck on an obstacle

Nussed: a nussed person is a spaced-out person

Ollie: skater uses the back foot to smack the tail of the board against the ground while the front foot pulls the board up into the air

O-vert: short for over vert, a transition that goes past vert so that the face of the transition is actually facing slightly down

Pickin up change: skater lands a set or a gap and slides his hand along the ground

Piss-pedaling: pumping mongo (skater pumping with his front foot instead of back foot)

Pop: the amount of snap and stiffness to a board; to smack the tail against the ground to initiate a trick

Popshove-it: the skater pops the board in the air where it rotates along its vertical axis

Poser: a nonskater who carries a board everywhere

Radical: excellent trick

Revert: skater finishes a trick coming out forwards, then quickly slides around 180 to come out backwards

Roll-in: part of the ramp that curves onto the platform

Sack-it: nut it; the skater lands on his jewels

Session: a skating session

Set: set of stairs

Shove-it: the board spins under the skater's feet without him turning his body

Sketchy: wobbly

Shibby: cool; state of coolness

Schralped: a few layers of skin removed

Slappy: grinding on curbs without ollieing them

Snakerun: twisting path

Stalefishgrab: grabbing the board behind you (around the back of your leg)

Steezy: skating with a combination of style and ease

Suspect: refers to uncertainty about whether skater executed trick appearing in a photo

TBC: Total Board Control

Technical: new skateboarders (vs. Old School skateboarders)

Thrashing: skater doing normal damage to the obstacle

Tic Tac: skater pivots left or right on his back wheels in order to accelerate or to land a trick off-center

Tranny: transition

Tricktionary—bag of tricks so sick they should be catalogued

Tweak: to add style by exaggerating or contorting

Varial: skater spins board along its vertical axis without popping the board in the air

Vert: vertical

Waxmark: the black residue left on obstacles

Wheelbite: occurs when too much weight is applied to one side of the board

Winding: skater twists hips and shoulders in order to get ready to spin or rotate

Glossary sources:

http://www.brockwaytwpskatepark.com/skatedictionary.htm
http://finalhoursskate.tripod.com/skatedictionary.com
http://www.skateboard-city.com
http://www.urbandictionary.com

Acknowledgments

The Collagist, The Cortland Review, Four Way Monthly (winner of Audio Poetry Contest), *Freight Stories, Hayden's Ferry Review, Huffpost 50, Iron Horse Literary Review, Kenyon Review Online, Missouri Review, New World Writing, Pif, Ploughshares, Prime Number, r.kv.r.y, Shadowgraph, Waxwing,* and *Western Humanities Review.*

Some of you miraculously stood by me during the crucial last years in which this book formed, and for all of it I owe you and will never be able to thank you adequately: Chris Hale, Tony Hoagland, Tom & Sue McIlvoy, Chris Burnham, Ann Rohovec, Kent Jacobs, Sallie Ritter, Miriam Altshuler, Don Mercer, Reed Turchi, Rachel Haley Himmelheber, Emilie White, Janet Shaw, Elizabeth Holden, Karen Brennan, Martha Rhodes, Reg Gibbons, Rus Bradburd, Don Kurtz, Darlin' Neal, Connie Voisine, Sebastian Matthews, Ellen Bryant Voigt, Robert Boswell, Peter Turchi, Amy Grimm, Rick Russo, Michael Collier, Patrick Donnelly, Brooks Haxton, Stacey D'Erasmo, C. J. Hribal, Alan Shapiro, Chuck Wachtel, Maurice Manning, Jennifer Grotz, Matthew Olzmann, Dale Neal, Stephen Dobyns, Joan Silber, Michael Martone, Evan Lavender-Smith, Deb Allbery, Sarah Stone, C. Dale Young, Debra Spark. I'm indebted to Sally Ball and Emily Price for brilliant editing guidance. Lillie Robertson provided me with a place to stay at an extremely difficult time in my life. Dr. Laurie LeMauviel helped keep me alive. Vermont Studio Center and Virginia Center for the Creative Arts gave me time inside. All of you who have trusted me for thirty-five years with your own poetry and fiction, thank you for teaching me the ways to leave the shore.

Kevin McIlvoy has published four novels, *A Waltz*, *The Fifth Station*, *Little Peg*, *Hyssop*, and a short story collection, *The Complete History of New Mexico*. His short fiction has appeared in *Harper's*, *Southern Review*, *Ploughshares*, *Missouri Review*, and other literary magazines. His short-short stories and prose poems have recently appeared in *The Collagist*, *The Cortland Review*, *Kenyon Review Online*, *New World Writing*, *Pif*, *Prime Number*, *r.kv.r.y*, *Shadowgraph*, and *Waxwing*. His novel, *At the Gate of All Wonder*, is forthcoming from Tupelo Press. He has received a National Endowment for the Arts Fellowship in fiction. For twenty-seven years he was fiction editor and editor-in-chief of the national literary magazine *Puerto del Sol*. He has taught in the Warren Wilson College MFA Program in Creative Writing since 1989; he taught as a Regents Professor of Creative Writing in the New Mexico State University English Department from 1981 to 2008. He served on the Board of Directors of the Council of Literary Magazines and Presses and the Association of Writers and Writing Programs. He mentors writers and edits full-length book manuscripts at mcthebookmechanic.com.

Publication of this book was made possible by grants and donations. We are also grateful to those individuals who participated in our 2016 Build a Book Program. They are:

Anonymous (8), Evan Archer, Sally Ball, Jan Bender-Zanoni, Zeke Berman, Kristina Bicher, Carol Blum, Lee Briccetti, Deirdre Brill, Anthony Cappo, Carla & Steven Carlson, Maxwell Dana, Machi Davis, Monica Ferrell, Martha Webster & Robert Fuentes, Dorothy Goldman, Lauri Grossman, Steven Haas, Mary Heilner, Henry Israeli, Christopher Kempf, David Lee, Jen Levitt, Howard Levy, Owen Lewis, Paul Lisicky, Katie Longofono, Cynthia Lowen, Louise Mathias, Nathan McClain, Gregory McDonald, Britt Melewski, Kamilah Aisha Moon, Carolyn Murdoch, Tracey Orick, Zachary Pace, Gregory Pardlo, Allyson Paty, Marcia & Chris Pelletiere, Eileen Pollack, Barbara Preminger, Kevin Prufer, Peter & Jill Schireson, Roni & Richard Schotter, Soraya Shalforoosh, Peggy Shinner, James Snyder & Krista Fragos, Megan Staffel, Marjorie & Lew Tesser, Susan Walton, Calvin Wei, Abigail Wender, Allison Benis White, and Monica Youn.